just another day in my insanely real life

A NOVEL BY BARBARA DEE

ALADDIN MIX
NEW YORK LONDON TORONTO SYDNEY

ALADDIN MIX
An imprint of Simon & Schuster Children's Publishing Division
1230 Avenue of the Americas, New York, NY 10020

Also available in a Margaret K. McElderry hardcover edition.
Designed by Sonia Chaghatzbanian
The text of this book was set in Proforma.
Manufactured in the United States of America
First Aladdin MIX edition April 2007
10 9 8 7 6 5 4 3 2 1
The Library of Congress has cataloged the hardcover edition as follows:
Dee, Barbara
Just another day in my insanely real life : a novel / by Barbara Dee.
1st ed.
p. cm.
Summary: With her father "out of the picture" and her mother working long hours, twelve-year-old Cassie unconsciously describes her anger and confusion in a fantasy novel she is writing for school.
ISBN-13: 978-1-4169-0861-6 (hc.)
ISBN-10: 1-4169-0861-7 (hc.)
[1. Authorship—Fiction. 2. Family problems—Fiction. 3. Brothers and sisters—Fiction. 4. Single-parent families—Fiction. 5. Schools—Fiction.] I. Title.
PZ7.D35867 Jus 2006
[Fic]—dc22
2005037515
ISBN-13: 978-1-4169-4739-4 (pbk.)
ISBN-10: 1-4169-4739-6 (pbk.)

For Alex, Josh, and Lizzy,
and especially for Chris

one

Cat aimed a precious poisoned arrow at the evil Lord Valdyk. "Put down your sword!" she commanded. "This arrow is dipped in dragonfire! If I shoot, you'll die at once!"

"Ah, but you won't shoot, Lady Catrain! Your father gave you only three such arrows! Just three! He intended that you use them only to defend Queen Alynna from gravest danger! (SUCH AS???) If you waste one of them on me, how do you intend to protect your Queen?"

"I'll still have two left, you snake!"

"Of course. But what if you miss? Will you use your second arrow against me, and leave yourself with but one?"

"I won't miss, you swine!"

"Don't be so sure, Lady Catrain. I've heard you're quite an impressive markswoman, but you are, after all, a mere girl. A girl with certain magical Gifts, but a girl nonetheless. And, as a girl, your hand may tremble, and your breath may shake. And then, my dear, if you shoot, you just might miss. Can you take that chance, Lady Catrain? Can you risk leaving your Queen virtually defenseless?"

Cat's green eyes flashed, and her red-gold hair grew fiery with anger. Lord Valdyk was right. She was a Gifted markswoman, but her training wasn't complete. If she missed, how could she defend her mother's throne from Lord Valdyk's men? She had no choice—she had to let Lord Valdyk go. But if she did, who knew what havoc the evil Lord might wreak (wreck?)?

"Cassie! What are you, brain-dead in there? Let's go!" screeched my lovely sister Miranda.

"Be there in a second," I sang back.

"Not in a second! *Now!*"

So, since I wasn't prepared for a full-scale war, which, frankly, was always an option when it came to interacting with my big sister, I re-capped my black extra-fine-point Rolling Writer, closed my regulation two-hundred-page college-lined spiral notebook, and went into the kitchen.

"What were you doing in there?" she grumbled.

"Homework. English."

"Yeah? Well, so sorry to interrupt, Miss Shakespeare, but it's your turn to make supper. Mom called. She said she'll be late, around eight thirty, so she'll pick up something on the way home from work. So just make something for you, me, and Jackson. Something *edible,* if you don't mind." Then she opened the freezer, took out a Chipwich, took a big bite, put the rest back in the freezer, slammed the freezer door, grabbed the phone, and started dialing.

"I hope that didn't ruin your supper, Young Lady," I said loudly, in my Authority Figure voice.

"I hope it did." She grinned evilly. Then she walked out.

So supper. I sighed. What in the world did I know about making supper? Nothing, completely zero. Usually when it was my turn, Mom left me directions straight out of *Microwaving for Morons* ("For lasagna, set microwave to five minutes. Use an oven mitt when you take it out—it's hot!!!"). But this morning she had a superearly "crisis" meeting and had to race out to catch the train. I opened the refrigerator and stared in. Mustard. Yessir, we had lotsa mustard. Honey mustard, spicy brown, country, dijon, tarragon. And a green relish kind that looked like cat barf.

"Randa!" I called. "Did you do the shopping?"

No answer.

I walked into the living room. Miranda was sprawled all over the couch, yakking on the phone.

"Excuse me for interrupting, Miranda, but did you do the shopping like you promised Mom, or *not*?"

"Just a minute, Madison," she said to Whoever, then rejoined the world of the upright. "Cassie, dear? Did you have a question or a comment?"

"Yeah. My question is, you forgot to do the shopping."

She stared at me. "Omigod," she said. "Omigod. Mad, gotta go. Yeah. Later, babe." She put the phone down. "Omigod, Cassie."

"Who's Madison?" I asked. "Isn't that the name of a street?"

"Avenue," Miranda said. "Listen, Cassie, I am so, so sorry. I just totally forgot *all* about the shopping, but you know I have this *killer* Math test tomorrow."

"And?"

"And I have a lot on my mind, okay? What do you want from me? I just said I'm really, really sorry. Isn't there anything else in the fridge?"

"There's . . . mustard. Oh, and some . . . mustard. And for dessert, there's . . . mustard."

"That's *all?*"

"Well, there's that Chipwich. We could split it three ways. What there's left of it."

Now Miranda glared at me. "Shut up, Cassandra. I told you I was sorry. I can't remember *everything*. What do you and Jackson want from me? I go to school too, you know."

Then Jackson came into the living room. "Can I tell you something? I'm hungry," he announced.

Miranda and I looked at each other.

"When's Mommy coming home?"

"Not till later," Miranda said.

"What time?"

"Later," Miranda repeated. She held out her hand.

"Let's go look in the kitchen for something to eat, Jackie."

"There's mustard," I suggested helpfully.

"Shut up," Miranda growled.

I followed them into the kitchen. I was *not* going to let Miranda off the hook. Now that Mom was working for a big law firm as Coordinator of Legal Support, whatever that meant, she was practically never home before seven during the school week. So Miranda was expected to pick up a few groceries on the way home from school, important stuff we ran out of, you know, like milk and bread. Mom usually did the big shopping after work on Friday, but this time was different: Grandpop had come down with a bad case of flu, so on Friday night we rushed up to his nursing home to be with him. Grandpop's really old and weak, and Mom was frantic there for a while, but by the end of the weekend his fever was almost normal, so we left. Then, as we pulled into our driveway at around ten on Sunday night, Mom suddenly groaned.

"Oh, no," she said. "I just realized. I was in such a hurry to see Grandpop on Friday that I never went shopping!"

"Oh, don't worry, Mom," Miranda said. "I'll take care of it tomorrow after school. Just write out a list and give me a blank check for the A & P."

"You sure?" Mom asked her, looking worried. "That's a lot for you to handle."

"No problem," Miranda said. "It's late, and you're tired. And nothing's open in town on Sunday night, anyway. I'm sure there's enough for breakfast. We'll be fine. Don't worry."

Then she kissed Mom's cheek. Miranda could be such a suck-up sometimes.

But the thing is, you couldn't believe a word she ever said. Not one single stupid, pathetic word. Did she actually do what she *offered* to do? Of course she didn't. And now here we were on Monday night, with a totally empty refrigerator, nothing but six different kinds of mustard for supper, and of course, guess what, it was now my problem.

Miranda opened the empty refrigerator, like she didn't believe me. "Great," she said.

She closed it. Then she looked in the pantry.

"Let's see," I announced, peering over her shoulder. "There's flour, baking soda, Tabasco, Cheerios, ranch dressing, stewed tomatoes, tea bags, maple syrup, canola oil, and Crisco. Oh, and iodized salt."

Miranda raised one eyebrow at me. "Got any money? We could order a pizza."

I reached into my jeans pocket and pulled out three crumpled dollar bills and some balled-up lint. "This is everything I've got. And anyway, I paid for the last three pizzas we ordered. Forget it, Ran."

"What? *You* didn't pay for them, *I* did! The last two, definitely! And I also paid for the Chinese food we ordered last Wednesday! Or did you conveniently forget that?"

"I'm *really, really* hungry!" Jackson wailed. The situation was clearly deteriorating.

"What about cereal?" I took the box of Cheerios from the pantry. It wouldn't be the first time we had Cheerios for supper, and I was pretty sure it wouldn't be the last.

But then Jackson started crying. "I want Mommy! I'm really hungry and I *hate* Cheerios, and I want Mommy to come home *right now!*"

Miranda picked him up. Jackson was almost six, the youngest in the family, and he got babied a lot. It disgusted me, if you want to know.

"Put him down," I said. "If he's really hungry, he'll eat Cheerios. It won't kill him."

"I HATE CHEERIOS!" Jackson shouted. "AND I HAVE A BOOK REPORT!"

Miranda put him down. "You have a *what?*"

"Book re-report," he hiccupped. "And I want Mommy to help me."

"But you're only in first grade," I protested. "How can they give you a book report? You can't even read!"

Miranda glared at me. "Yes, he can, Cassbrain. Remember the Bob book he brought home last week?"

"He memorized it, Ran!"

Now Jackson started wailing again.

"Well, I totally can't deal with this," Miranda announced. "Cassie, if you want to eat Cheerios, eat Cheerios. I'll be in my room studying." And then she took the rest of the Chipwich from the freezer and flounced down the hallway to her room.

So, it was me and Jackson.

"Listen, Jackie," I said. "Here's the deal. You can have Cheerios for supper, or mustard. Miranda forgot to do the shopping, so those are the choices. What'll it be?"

"Cheerios," he sniffed.

I poured us each a bowl.

"With milk," he said.

"No milk," I said calmly. "Miranda forgot to buy milk. Would you like some mustard in your Cheerios, señor?"

Now he started to giggle. "No way, José."

"Okeydokey. So we'll eat 'em raw." Now that he'd stopped acting like a baby, I was ready to goof around.

But then, all of a sudden, he started crying again. "BUT WHAT ABOUT MY BOOK REPORT?"

I just stared at him, my mouth full of dusty Cheerios. "Listen, Jackie, Miranda is very busy studying, and I have a ton of homework myself. I really can't help you with this. And Mom won't be back until after your bedtime."

Jackson was silent for a second. Then he stuck out his lower lip and dumped his bowl of Cheerios on the floor.

"WHAT DID YOU JUST DO?" I shouted.

Now he was wailing again.

"CASSANDRA, KEEP IT DOWN OUT THERE! I TOLD YOU I'M STUDYING!" Miranda screeched.

"WELL, GUESS WHAT! I HAVE HOMEWORK TOO!" I yelled back. I turned to Jackson. "Okay, buddy. You'd better pick up every single one of these Cheerios. I'm going back in my room, and when I get out, if there's a single Cheerio on the floor, you'll be sorry!"

Jackson was whimpering as he got on his knees to pick up all three trillion Cheerio smithereens one by one. Part of me felt guilty for being so mean to him, but I knew I had every right to be angry. There was no food in the house, Miranda had bailed out, and I was stuck taking care of a bratty, overgrown baby with a stupid book report. And I was in the middle of work of my own.

Lord Valdyk laughed. He knew he had Cat paralyzed, trapped in the hungry quicksand of her terrible dilemma. Destroy her evil nemesis, (who? whom?) she had labored so hard and so long to face at last? Or let the evil Lord go, preserving the three precious arrows to defend the Queen?

Just then, little Daeman, Cat's distant cousin and constant shadow, came running into the Grand Meeting Hall. "Cat! Cat! There's a problem! Someone broke into the Queen's Stable and stole two prize warhorses! You must come at once!"

"It will have to wait, Daeman," Cat replied. "I have more pressing matters to attend to right now." She kept the arrow pointing at Valdyk, but she could feel her fingers starting to tremble. Stay focused, she told herself. Forget the horses.

But just then Daeman realized that Cat was aiming her poisoned arrow at the evil Lord Valdyk. The small boy panicked, backing frantically into the Queen's Battle Map, which suddenly came crashing to the floor.

"Daeman! What have you done!" cried Cat. She stared at the ruined Battle Map, the little pins (signifying royal army units) scattered all over the polished floor.

"Ha!" triumphed Valdyk. "Let's see the Queen's battle plans now!"

"Cassie? Can I tell you something?"

"What is it?"

"I finished."

"Finished what?"

"The Cheerios. I picked them all up."

I stared at Jackson. He looked pathetic, pale and red-eyed. And small. Really, really small. Suddenly I felt incredibly sorry for him. "Thanks, Jackie. Now go put on your pj's, okay?"

"So early?"

"It's not early. It's almost eight."

"Oh. Okay. Cassie?"

"What?"

"I'm sorry."

"That's okay. I'm sorry too."

"For what?"

"For yelling at you. I'll tell Mom about the book report, and she'll work on it with you tomorrow."

"That's when it's due!"

"Yeah? Well, your teacher will understand. Don't worry."

Jackson's lip began to tremble. "But what if Mom's working late tomorrow night too?"

"Then *I'll* help you. Or Miranda will. Stop worrying so much! Now please just get into your pj's and brush your teeth, okay?"

"Okay. Cassie?"

"*What?*"

"Buster and Fuzzy are hungry. I think they want some cat food."

I slammed my spiral notebook shut. Was I expected to do everything, solve every single domestic crisis around here?

"MIRANDA!" I yelled down the hall.

"WHAT IS IT!"

"DID YOU FORGET TO BUY CAT FOOD?"

"WAS IT ON THE SHOPPING LIST?"

How should I know? Mom made the list for *her*, not me. "YEAH!"

"THEN I DIDN'T BUY IT! I DIDN'T *GO* SHOPPING, REMEMBER?"

I stormed into her room. "Well, the cats are starving, and we can't exactly give them Cheerios and mustard, can we?"

She shrugged dramatically.

"That's it? That's all you have to say?"

Now she sighed dramatically. "Cassandra darling, I already *told* you, like, five thousand times that I'm sorry. What exactly do you want me to do?"

"Get the stupid cat food!"

"Get it yourself."

I stared at her in disbelief. "How? It's eight o'clock at night!"

"So? The CVS is open twenty-four hours. It's not too far. Take your bike."

"But it's your fault! Why should I have to go?"

"Cassie," she said patiently, as if she were explaining things to a retarded toddler with a long-term memory problem. "This is *not* my fault. None of it. It's *Dad's* fault for leaving us, and forcing Mom to be out working at all hours. I am not a housewife, I am a hardworking student trying to get the best possible grade in Math so I can go to the college of my choice and get *out* of this madhouse, and if I forgot to buy cat food, I am just very sorry for the *ten millionth time*, but if *you* want to go out at night and go shopping, it's *fine with me!*"

"FINE!" I roared. Then I grabbed my sweatshirt, crammed my three dollars into the front pocket, got my bike, and zoomed out of the house.

two

It wasn't always like this, but sometimes that's hard to believe. Sometimes I have to remind myself that back in the days when Dad was with us, we were like every other family in Emerson: nice house, big backyard, two cars, a zillion after-school activities, vacations at Disneyland, once even a ski trip to Utah.

Then something happened. I was never sure what. All I knew was that sometime early last spring Mom and Dad started having what they called "private discussions." I'd go into a room and there they'd be, glaring at each other, not saying a word. "Cassie, dear, could you give us a moment," Mom would say. "Dad and I are having a *private discussion.*"

"Okay, sure, no problem," I'd mutter, wondering how you could have a discussion when you weren't even talking.

And then one day in May, Mom announced at dinner that Dad was "out of the picture." I was eleven and a half and scared; I kept imagining all our family photos with Dad's face just gone, like there was a digital photo god somewhere keeping track of families and then systematically deleting people who one day just weren't there anymore. Miranda was almost fifteen, so she felt like she had the right to keep asking Mom questions. But all Mom would ever say to her was, "I really don't know Dad's plans right now, but I'll tell you when I do." Which, according to Miranda, meant: "Dad is 'out of the picture,' so just deal with it, Miranda."

Mom spent a lot of time in her bedroom, and I heard her crying all the time, so I kept out of her way and acted like everything was just fine. Besides, I thought, if she wasn't telling Dad's "plans" to Miranda, why would she tell me? Once I saw her accept a registered letter from Florida, so my theory was that Dad had moved down there for some reason. I didn't know this for sure: He'd called us exactly five times since May, but "to hear our voices," he said, not to tell us what was going on. The last three times he called were back in August, and every time, Miranda just hung up on him.

So then everything changed. We had to sell our nice big house and our second car, quit our activities, start counting every penny. Mom wanted to stay in Emerson because, she said, we were "doing so well in the schools." So we moved into a "unit" in Shady Woods, a ratty old condo development on the edge of town. (I don't mean ratty in the sense that it had actual rats; I mean ratty in the sense that it was old and kind of shabby.) It's where all the divorced parents go when their families break up. Usually one parent keeps the nice big house where the kids live, and then the kids visit the other parent's ratty little "unit" on weekends. (Usually the dad gets the "unit," but our next-door neighbor, Mrs. Patella, was a mom, so it can go either way, I guess. Of course, Mrs. Patella's kids were all grown up, so she doesn't really count, anyway.) As far as I knew, we were the only family living in a "unit" full-time, and I hated everything about it: the tiny square rooms, the thin walls, the concrete outside instead of our old backyard. But I also knew we were lucky to have it, so I didn't complain, except in my head, and then only when I was feeling really grouchy.

The other big thing that changed was that now Mom was at work *all* the time, instead of just *part* of the time, like she was when Dad was "in the picture." Last May when Dad left, Mom hired this nice housekeeper-slash-nanny (housekeeper for Miranda and me, nanny for Jackson). Her name was Sophie Kwidzyn and she was from Kraków, Poland, and cooked this weird food that actually tasted pretty good. Miranda was kind of snotty to her, but Jackson *loved* her. He followed her around the "unit" like a big-eyed puppy and crawled into her lap whenever she sat down. She hugged and kissed him and called him all these words in Polish that sounded like creamy desserts.

Then at the beginning of September, a few days before school was about to start, Sophie told Mom that she had to go back to Kraków to take care of her sick father. "Two weeks," she promised, "and then I come back." But two weeks passed, and then three, and no Sophie. Mom finally phoned her in Poland and found out that she wasn't coming back, not in two weeks, not ever. Jackson, of course, freaked out. Mom was frantic—she had to get back to work to Coordinate Legal Support, but who would watch Jackson? Aunt Abby came to help out for a few days, but she had to get back to her own family. Mom tried hiring a bunch of different babysitters from some babysitter agency, but Jackson hated every single one and just kept crying and crying for Sophie. I was starting to lose it, being stuck in this ratty little "unit" with all these strange women trying to calm down a hysterical little brother and a furious teenage sister playing "music" as loud as she could to drown out the noise. Finally, when I was *this close* to going psycho, Miranda called a family meeting.

"Listen," she told Mom. "This is crazy. I'm fifteen years old, I've been babysitting since I was twelve, and I'm not moving back to Kraków. So, why can't I just watch Jackson in the afternoons until you get home?"

Mom looked surprised, but not shocked. "That's nice of you to offer, sweetheart," she said slowly, "but it's a big responsibility. Jackson needs a lot of attention. What about your homework?"

"I'll be good!" Jackson swore. He looked like a puppy desperate for a bone.

"Of course, baby, you're always good," Mom said, kissing his cheek, "but I don't know."

"Jackie plays by himself all the time, anyway," Miranda continued. "He'll be quiet, so I'm sure I'll be able to study. And Cassie will help, won't you, Cassie?" She stared at me with a bright *Say yes* smile.

"Oh, sure," I said. Jackie sure seemed to want it. Anyway, what could be worse than what was already going on around here?

"*And* you won't have to pay me, so we'll save money," Miranda said.

Mom looked upset. "Miranda, that's not the issue!"

"Of course," Miranda agreed. "But if you *want* to pay me . . ."

"I'm not going to pay you for helping out!"

"Fine," said Miranda. "So let me help out. At least give it a few weeks."

That clinched it. And for the first couple of weeks it worked fine, definitely better than with the strange women and all the crying. Miranda would give Jackson a big hug when he got off the school bus, pour him some Nesquik, hang out with him for a few minutes, then do her homework while he played Power Rangers in his room or watched TV. At six she and I would take turns microwaving supper, and then Mom was usually home by seven. Things were almost normal, I thought. But by the end of a month Miranda was turning back into her old irresponsible, lazy, selfish self, and so here I was out on a school night, bicycling four blocks to the CVS.

I never liked biking at night, and now that it was late October the nights were chilly. But I had no choice: If I didn't buy the cat food, Miranda sure wouldn't, and then the cats would declare war, chewing on my spiral notebook, knocking books off the shelves, scratching up my desk, meowing. And then, if all that failed, barfing. Buster and Fuzzy could barf at will. They would barf if they didn't get fed, didn't get brushed, didn't get petted. Once they barfed right in my slippers during the night so I felt a nice cold squoosh when I put them on in the morning. And every day they would barf for their breakfast at precisely six thirty-four a.m., a full one minute *before* my alarm clock went off at six thirty-five. There was *no way* they'd let me survive the night if they didn't get fed. And if I didn't feed them, I knew, nobody would.

The CVS was lit up like a maximum-security prison as I coasted into the parking lot. Oh, great, I thought: I hadn't brought my bicycle lock. Well, I'd only be in the store for a minute. I parked my bike right in front of the door, raced inside to Aisle 8, Pet Supplies, and grabbed four slightly dented cans of Friskies Turkey & Giblets Dinner. That sure sounded better than Cheerios & Mustard Dinner. Suddenly it occurred to me that unless I got some milk, tomorrow morning we'd be having Cheerios & Mustard Breakfast.

So I raced over to Aisle 1, where they kept the milk: big, sweaty full gallons of Dairyland's Delight. *Shhhheeetrock!* There was no way I could ride a bike carrying a gallon of milk; a quart, maybe, but definitely not a gallon. I stuck my arm way in the back of the sour-smelling refrigerator, hoping that maybe an almost-expired quart of milk would be lurking somewhere, when suddenly I heard someone say, "Cassie? Is that you?"

I spun around. Oh, *fabulous.* "Hi, Mrs. Langley."

Mrs. Langley was our old neighbor when we lived in a house, not a ratty little "unit." She had two little Yorkies that liked to pee on our grass. They had incredibly stupid names: Honey and Sugar.

"I almost didn't recognize you! You've gotten so big!" she gushed.

"Thanks," I said, as if I'd done it on purpose.

"Is your mother here?" she asked, looking around.

"Uh, no. She's home. She just realized we're short of milk, so I volunteered to pick some up."

"On a school night? What a wonderful daughter you are! But how did you get here? Did you walk?"

My heart started to beat fast, but I wasn't sure why. What was wrong with buying some milk at eight (now eight twenty, actually) on a Monday night? Nothing. And it was none of her business how I got here. I opened the refrigerator and hauled out a gallon of whole milk. We never drank whole milk, and I wasn't sure how I'd carry a gallon, but now I just wanted to get away from Mrs. Langley.

"Okay, well, nice to see you, bye!" I called out as I escaped to the checkout line. Of course, I knew it was rude to just stop talking to her, not even answering her question, but it wasn't like she was still our neighbor, and she wasn't even our friend. I once heard Mom telling Aunt Abby how ever since we'd moved into the ratty little "unit," lots of people just cut us off. Like we were tainted or something, just because Dad was "out of the picture" and we had no money. Miranda kept her friends because she spent all her time yakking on the phone, but I was pretty positive that my two so-called best friends, Hayley Garrison and Brianna Schuster, had written me off just because I dropped swim team at the fitness club. They still talked to me at school and everything, but not like before.

"NEXT!" barked the cashier. I put the gallon of milk and the four cans of cat food on the counter.

"Find everything you want today?" he said, yawning.

"Yup."

"Would you like to receive our online newsletter about in-store discounts and other promotions?"

"I'd really just like to pay," I said under my breath.

"Sure thing," he said. He scanned my stuff. "Five twenty-nine." He yawned again.

Monkey droppings! All I'd brought was three dollars! "Um, forget about the milk, then," I mumbled.

But Mrs. Langley had caught up with me. She tapped me on the shoulder. "Cassie, dear, are you short?"

I stood there with my back to her. I shook my head.

"I don't mean *short*," she apologized. "I mean *short of cash*."

Now I turned around. My face was burning. *"I'm fine,"* I practically growled.

Then I plunked down the three dollars, grabbed the cans of cat food, got back on my bike, and zoomed home.

three

"Cassie? That you?"

I went into the living room. "Mom?"

"I'm just reading with Jackson. I'll be out in a sec!" she called. I heard her in Jackson's room saying something, then Jackson giggling, then smoochy good-night kisses. Finally she came out into the living room, still wearing her office costume.

"Miranda said you went out for cat food. Thank you, honey, but I'd really rather you weren't out bicycling at night. It's dangerous."

"Listen, Mom," I protested, "it's a lot more dangerous facing the wrath of Buster and Fuzzy!"

She gave a tired laugh. "Okay. But I don't want you out at night when I'm not home. I don't want you out at night, period."

That made two of us. "Fine," I said.

"So, what did you make for supper tonight?" she asked. I could see Miranda lurking outside the living room, listening. *Don't tell her,* she mouthed frantically.

"Um, actually, I didn't. I was really busy doing homework, so we just ordered pizza," I said. All things considered, it was probably best not to rat on Miranda about the shopping. It's not like I was this insanely loyal supersister who would never betray her own kind—I was actually furious with Miranda for a million things, most recently for exposing me to Mrs. Langley's nosy questions. But at that moment I decided that if I kept Miranda's little shopping omission a secret, I might be able to cash in later, sometime when I really needed to.

Thank you! Miranda mouthed.

"Pizza? Again?" Mom screwed up her face. "First of all, it's not the most nutritious thing in the world, and second of all, it's expensive."

"It's not so bad," I protested. "It has protein and calcium. And I used a three-dollars-off coupon, so it was only seven dollars for a pie."

Miranda gave me two thumbs-up signs. *I love you,* she mouthed.

Mom was too tired to argue. "Okay. But no more pizza for a week. I mean it. How did your homework go?"

"Fine. But I haven't finished writing in my journal for English."

"Oh, how's that going? Has Mr. Mullaney checked it yet?"

"Nope. The first journal check is next week."

"Okay. Well, it's late, sweetheart. Why don't you go wash up for bed?"

"Can I just write a little more in my journal? I'm almost done." For English we were supposed to write five single-spaced pages a week. Mr. Mullaney was the most nasty, sarcastic, *boring* English teacher in the whole seventh grade, but at least he let us write anything we wanted in our journals, as long as we filled those pages. It was a lot of work, but lately it was the only school thing I really cared about. I was totally into this Cat versus Valdyk story, even if I didn't have a clue where it was going.

"Okay. I'll give you ten minutes. And maybe sometime when you're ready, you'll show me this story you're working on?"

"Sure!" Mom was pretty cool. She wasn't one of those mothers who'd roll her eyes at all the battle stuff, and feel like she had to remind you all the time how she didn't approve of violence. I mean, who did? Besides, this was a fantasy, not real life, and fantasies absolutely *had* to have a certain amount of swordfights and dragon battles and poison arrows. And anyway, Catrain was a noble heroine who used her dragonfire arrows as a totally last resort, and only to serve her Queen. To tell you the truth, I hadn't written a scene where she actually used one, and I wasn't even sure I would.

I kissed Mom's cheek. It seemed kind of deflated, like she'd lost weight, which wouldn't be surprising, considering how hard she was working. I wanted to say something, but I couldn't think of what: *Mom, are you okay? Mom, thanks for working so hard. Mom, don't worry.* None of it sounded right. So, I just went into the kitchen where Buster and Fuzzy were circling their food dishes and screeching, *Feed us, feed us, feed us!*

"Okay, you little beasts," I scolded. "Calm down!" I opened a dented can of Turkey & Giblets and dumped it into a crusty bowl, last washed sometime on Saturday. They didn't care; they dove in. At least someone around here was having a real supper, I thought, sighing as I remembered the gallon of milk I'd deserted back at the CVS. Breakfast was going to stink too.

I went down the hallway to my room. Miranda was sitting on my bed, brushing her shampoo-smelling long brown hair.

"You're in my room," I said.

"Bravo, Captain Obvious." She grinned.

"So get out."

"I will, in a second. I just wanted to thank you for saying we had pizza."

"Okay," I snarled. "But you'd better go shopping tomorrow."

"I will, I promise! I'm setting my alarm to go off at five a.m., and then I'll go to the A & P before school. We'll have a ton of stuff for breakfast, I swear!"

I sat on my bed. "We'd better. Because I have a feeling Mom is going to catch on when she wants breakfast and there's nothing to eat but spicy brown mustard."

"Okay, Cassie. I get it! *Okay!*"

"Fine. Great. So get out, Miranda. And shut the door."

I sat down at my desk and opened my spiral notebook.

Cat mounted her beloved stallion, Starlight, and set out to search for the Queen's two prize warhorses. Only someone close to the Queen could have broken into the stable, she thought, but who? Was there a traitor within the castle walls, someone secretly plotting with Valdyk? Cat was Gifted—she could see and hear things others could not—but she still couldn't imagine who the traitor could be.

Despite her worries, it felt great to be galloping through the dark forest, the wind flowing in her long, red-gold hair. Yes, she had let Valdyk get away, but it was really for the best. The King had warned her about Valdyk before he left to hunt the Mystyck Beast. "Just hold the fort, my Catrain," he had smiled, his eyes twinkling. "Let me deal with this miserable knave when I return." Anyway, she told herself, Lord Valdyk wasn't worth losing one of her precious three dragonfire arrows over. Those three arrows were all she had, and all her magical Gifts couldn't get her any more.

The important thing was staying focused. The realm was full of evil, full of mischief. Valdyk's spies were everywhere, waiting to attack, hungry for damaging information about the

Queen. But she would never divulge the Queen's whereabouts, no matter how hard she was pressed. Though she was only fifteen (sixteen? seventeen?) and, as Lord Valdyk put it, a mere girl, Catrain was all that stood between the Queen's throne and total chaos.

I was exhausted; I couldn't finish writing. *Oh, well,* I thought. Mr. Mullaney wasn't checking the journals until next week, anyway. I'd finish the chapter tomorrow, after a good long sleep, curled up in my bed with Fuzzy and Buster, who were finally quiet and well fed and cuddly and purring. *I love my cats,* I thought, nestling beside them. Dog people thought cats were aloof and self-centered, but I knew better: Once you got to know them, cats were loyal and sensitive and fun and snuggly, maybe even the best friends I had.

four

Hggaah! Hhhgggaaaaah!

The retching noise was unmistakable. Yuck. Nothing like the sound of barfing cat to start your day.

"BUSTER! FUZZY! CUT IT OUT!" I yelled. Precisely thirty seconds later my clock radio went off: "And in national news the president announced—" I slammed the snooze button and bolted upright, dizzy. Just another glorious day.

The floor was cold, so I kicked my slippers out from under my bed, inspecting them first. Phew. No barf. The cats had only barfed there once, but once was enough to make you check forever. Probably I'll be ninety-five years old and still checking my orthopedic slippers for cat barf.

I shuffled down the hall, past the wet blob of cat spit outside Miranda's room. Then I heard another disgusting sound, right up there with cat barf: the sound of Miranda snoring.

You have to understand how hungry I still was after having nothing to eat the night before but Cheerios. I mean, my stomach was growling almost as loudly as Miranda was snoring, which was like a cross between a snorting warthog and a leaf blower. I've always thought that snoring was a stupid sound; I can't imagine Einstein snoring, and Miranda snoring just seemed to totally prove how stupid she was. But this morning the sound of snoring was worse than just stupid. It meant that Miranda hadn't gotten up at five like she'd promised, hadn't gone to the A & P, hadn't shopped for food. It meant a Cheerios & Mustard Breakfast, which this morning I absolutely could not deal with.

So I shuffled back into my bedroom. After barfing up his daily constitutional hairball, Buster had taken off, but Fuzzy was still curled up on my bed like a tortoiseshell Frisbee. I scooped him up. He immediately started purring, so I gave him a kiss.

Then I walked into Miranda's bedroom, and dumped Fuzzy on her head.

"Hey! Blah! What was that!" she screeched, wiping her

tongue as Fuzzy scampered away. Apparently she'd gotten fur in her mouth. Way to go, Fuzzy.

"It's six forty," I announced.

"So?"

"*So*, weren't you supposed to get up at five? Didn't you swear to me last night that you'd go buy us breakfast this morning?"

She sat up in bed and stared. "Omigod. Cassie, omigod. I am so, so sorry!"

"Yeah? Well, I am so, so hungry."

"Me too," she said. "I don't know what happened! My alarm must be broken or something." She actually did look miserable at that moment. Miserable and confused. And hungry.

"At least you had a Chipwich," I reminded her. Then all my anger just dissolved. I don't know why, but all of a sudden it just seemed pointless to be having this discussion. Miranda was hopeless.

I turned to leave her room. "Where are you going?" she demanded.

"To get dressed for school. They sell bagels in the cafeteria if you get there early enough."

"But you said you have no money."

"I don't. I'll put it on my lunch account. Tell Mom when she gets out of the shower."

"What'll I say?"

I didn't even bother to answer that. *Let Miranda figure out something for a change,* I thought. Then I slipped on my old red sweater and my least grungy jeans, scrunchied my unshampooed hair into a ponytail, went into the kitchen to feed the cats (*Feed us! Feed us! Feed us!*), grabbed my backpack, and went out to unlock my bike.

But I didn't get past the first step. There on the bottom step of our ratty little "unit" was a huge wicker basket crammed with pink cellophane. Stapled onto the pink cellophane was a little yellow envelope.

I ripped it open. On a little yellow note card was a message written in a big puffy script:

Good morning, Baldwin family! I thought these goodies looked so scrumptious in the bakery that I couldn't resist!! I hope you have a lovely breakfast!! See you soon!!!

Fondly,
Joanna Langley

At first I didn't get it. Then I did: This was a care package from Mrs. Langley. She was lavishing pity on us because Dad was "out of the picture" and we were living in a ratty little "unit" and were too "short of cash" to buy a stupid gallon of milk at CVS. Oh, *cat barf.* I picked up the basket, which was surprisingly heavy, and hauled it into our kitchen as fast as I could so that nosy Mrs. Patella next door wouldn't see it.

I plunked it on the table. It must have weighed twenty pounds.

"What's that?" challenged Miranda, who was already in the kitchen, probably to fix herself a bowl of delicious Cheerios.

I narrowed my eyes at her. "Nothing."

"Don't tell me it's nothing! It looks like a gift basket! Who's it from?" She grabbed the little yellow card. "Joanna Langley? Our old neighbor? With the Yorkies?"

"Yeah."

"I don't get it. Why should she send us a gift basket? We haven't seen her since we moved."

"It's not a present, Miranda. It's a care package!"

"What are you talking about?" she demanded as she removed the pink cellophane. Inside the basket were four big gorgeous blueberry muffins, three huge crusty bagels, some French pastries that looked like miniature floats in a Thanksgiving Day parade, a pint-size container of cream cheese, three Golden Delicious apples, three oranges, and a bunch of bananas. Oh, yeah: and a gallon of Dairyland's Delight.

"Oh. My. God," Miranda gasped.

"Listen, we can't accept this," I hissed. "It's *charity*! Mom will kill us!"

"Cassie, you're delusional. Why in the world would Mrs. Langley send us charity?"

Just then, Jackson walked into the kitchen. His eyes were enormous, as if he thought he might be dreaming. "What's this? Breakfast?"

Miranda stared at me with raised eyebrows and a little smirk, as if to ask, *Do YOU want to tell this poor starving child that he can't accept this so-called charity? Huh?*

I sank into a chair. "What'll we tell Mom?" I asked lamely.

Miranda shrugged. "I went shopping?" she suggested, selecting a blueberry muffin and taking a huge bite.

"I want one of those cake things," Jackson said, pointing. "The one with the cream."

Miranda smiled at me graciously, like she'd baked

this stuff herself. "Cassie? What about you?"

"Nothing."

"Oh, come on, have something! If she wants to be nice, let her. She can afford it."

"Who? If who wants to be nice?" Jackson asked, licking the cream.

"Nobody, Jackie," Miranda said. "Besides, it's the least she can do after all those years of letting her dogs pee on our grass."

"Who?" Jackson demanded. *"What grass?"*

"Nobody's," I grumbled. "And what about Mom?"

"What *about* Mom?" Mom asked, walking into the kitchen in her office costume. She had obviously just put on her office perfume, and now the kitchen stank like Chanel.

She eyed the basket. "What's all this?"

I sighed. If I explained to Mom why Mrs. Langley had sent the basket, then I'd have to explain about the gallon of milk at the checkout line, thereby exposing Miranda's negligence, thereby losing me any tactical advantage I might have in future confrontations. Besides, last night was the time to tell Mom about the shopping, not now. I'd already told her we'd had pizza for supper because I was too busy to cook; if I told her the *real* reason I couldn't cook, she'd just blame me for lying to her last night. I definitely didn't have the stomach to go through all that. And anyway, it was getting late, and I'd probably already missed all the decent bagels at school.

"It's nothing, Mom," I said. "I ran into Mrs. Langley last night when I went to get cat food. She probably sent this over because she feels guilty she never visited us."

Mom half-smiled. "Pretty late for a housewarming gift," she commented. "Anyway, that was nice of her. How's that muffin, Miranda?"

Miranda smiled angelically. "Amazing. Have one." She chose a big muffin bursting with wet blueberries and put it on a cake plate. "For you, madame."

Suck-up.

"Yum," said Mom. "Thank you, honey. Cassie, aren't you having any?"

"No," I said. "I'm not." But then I decided: Mrs. Langley owed me the milk. The muffins and the pastries and the fruit I absolutely couldn't eat, but for some strange reason I was convinced that she owed me that milk. So I got out the big box of Cheerios, poured myself a bowlful, and then drenched it in Dairyland's Delight.

"Cassie, are you crazy?" Miranda cried. "How can you eat that?"

"Don't you want to try this? It's great," Jackson said, holding out his Thanksgiving Day float.

I munched my cereal grimly. "I'm *fine.*"

"We'll have to send Mrs. Langley a thank-you card," Mom said.

"I'll take care of it," I snapped. "Why not? I take care of everything else!" Then, before I even knew what I was doing, I got up from the table, grabbed my backpack, and slammed the kitchen door behind me.

five

"Catrain, I cannot conceal my displeasure," said Queen Alynna. "You had Valdyk in your control, and you let him go? How could you blunder so badly?"

Catrain's big sister, Princess Gloriana, was smiling as she fingered her elegant lute. She loved it when Cat got in trouble. It happened rarely, but when it did, Gloriana always celebrated.

"I did it for you," Cat stammered.

"For me?"

"Yes, Your Majesty. I thought that if I shot Valdyk, I might waste one of the three dragon-fire arrows that the King gave me. Then what would I use if Valdyk's army was invading? Or if the Mystyck Beast was attacking? I couldn't take that chance!"

The Queen shook her noble head. "Nothing is more important than vanquishing Valdyk. Nothing. Your bad judgment may have cost us the throne. Look at this."

The Queen's sorcerer, Zed, waved his hand over a magical hand-mirror. Instantly there appeared an image of the Mystyck Beast heading toward the castle, followed by Valdyk and his army on horseback.

"Look at that horse Valdyk is riding!" Gloriana gasped. "It's one of the two missing warhorses! How did he get them?"

"It little matters. They're heading this way, daughters," said Queen Alynna grimly. "And now we must ready ourselves for their attack."

"So, Cassie, how about number two?"

I blinked. Unless Mr. Mullaney was referring to a number two pencil, which at that moment I was using to scribble in my journal, I had nothing to offer him.

"I'm sorry?" I said.

"Sorry for what? For not attending, or for being impolite?"

Was he giving me a choice? I wish. Mr. Mullaney was always doing that Socratic thing, where the teacher pretends he's teaching by just asking a lot of questions. Usually he had a "right" answer already picked out in his head anyway, and he just kept asking until someone guessed what he was thinking. Or he'd give you two bogus "choices," and zap you if you guessed the "wrong" one. I never bothered guessing, because what was the point? Mr. Mullaney just plain hated me, and he hated everything I ever said.

And why? Because I daydreamed while he plodded through our *boring* grammar book, which the other seventh-grade teachers didn't even bother to use? Because I refused to study for our weekly spelling tests, which were like baby, elementary-school, mindless exercises in memorization? Because I once complained that he never even assigned us a real book to read, just gave us excerpts from some "fiction textbook" that wasn't even published, that was just a bunch of stupid loose sheets of paper that kept falling out of my notebook and getting lost?

The bell rang. I was almost saved. But no. "Cassie, don't you think you should stay in at lunch today and finish your grammar exercise?" Mr. Mullaney sneered. "Everyone else, be sure to study for tomorrow's quiz. Remember: 'Whom' is a direct object! 'Who' is a subject! Class dismissed!"

Hayley Garrison flashed me a sympathetic look. "Poor you," she said softly. Then she whispered something to Brianna Schuster. I pretended not to notice; I re-scrunchied my ponytail, then just kept writing in my journal.

"But what can we do to stop them?" Gloriana gasped.

"Maybe nothing," the Queen frowned. "But for now, I'm dispatching Sir Wyfryd (Gryfyd? Clyfyd?) and his men to meet them at the gate."

Gloriana glowed. She hoped one day to marry handsome Sir Wyfryd (whoever). If he could succeed here, it would ensure that he would be promoted to Lord Wyfryd (whatever), and be granted a castle of his own. Gloriana hoped to move into that castle, as his lovely bride.

Cat nearly exploded. "But, Your Majesty! How can you put Sir Wyfryd (?) in charge of such an important assignment?"

"Why not, Catrain? Do you know of any reason why he should not be entrusted with this job?"

Yes, she did, of course. Sir Wyfryd (?) didn't care one iota about the Queen's plight. Also, his swordsmanship stank (RE-WORD!). But after letting Valdyk go so stupidly, what could she say? That the Queen should have given her the job? She was lucky that the Queen wasn't taking away her dragonfire arrows and making her play the lute.

"As for you, Catrain," said the Queen. "I think you should remain in the castle for a while. Maybe you could teach Daeman, (whom? who?) I have recently neglected, how to shoot arrows at feather pillows."

"Yes, Your Majesty," Cat replied. So she was being punished, after all! And for what! For trying to protect the Queen! It definitely wasn't fair!

six

Since our food-free refrigerator kind of got in the way of my bringing lunch from home, first I had to go to the cafeteria to get something to eat. Normally the thought of having to eat lunch with Mr. Mullaney would make me lose my appetite, but today, for obvious Miranda-related reasons, I was starving. So I got in the Cheeseburger/Taco Burger/Fries line, which ran parallel to the Healthy Foods line, currently populated exclusively by Bess Waterbury, the fattest girl in the seventh grade.

"Hi, Cassie," she said shyly.

"Hi."

"Mr. Mullaney sure is a jerk," she said.

"Yup."

"I'm sorry he was so mean to you."

"Thanks."

It was her turn to get lunch. She took a container of strawberry yogurt and an apple, and carefully put them on her tray. This I didn't understand. Every day she would take something tiny and virtuous and low fat, and still she must have weighed, like, two hundred pounds. How was this possible? Did she stuff her face in private? I didn't like to think about it; to be honest, I didn't like to think about her at all, even though she was always trying to talk to me.

Now it was my turn. Today I was feeling sorry for myself, so I felt entitled to treat myself to whatever looked good. Besides, it was entirely possible that Miranda would screw up *again* and there'd be nothing to eat when I got home, so I knew I should pig out while I could. Taco burger, chicken nuggets, fries, a yogurt sundae: That should hold me until breakfast tomorrow.

I took my tray to the scanner. "Nine seventy-three," the cafeteria aide announced. "You've overdrawn your account by two dollars and ten cents."

"I'll tell my mom," I muttered, scanning the cafeteria to see where Hayley and Brianna were sitting. They were at the table right near Danny Abbott, a boy I sort of liked, so my first thought was to sit anywhere else. But then Hayley saw me and waved me over.

"My *God,*" she cried, staring at my tray. "Cassie, have you developed some kind of eating disorder or something?"

"You sure that's not O-Bess Waterbury's lunch?" Brianna giggled. Hayley laughed too. Danny's back was to us, so I couldn't tell if he was listening or not.

"Hey, come on, Brianna, don't call her that," I said. "I really hate it."

"Yes, *we know, we know.* Next time we'll ask your permission, we promise!"

"No, I'm serious. You should give her a break. She didn't do anything to you."

She smirked. "Cassie Baldwin, Defender of the Weak!"

I salted my chicken nuggets. Then I popped one in my mouth. "Shut up, Brianna," I said.

Hayley and Brianna exchanged a look.

"So, anyway, aren't you supposed to be having lunch with Mr. Mullaney?" Hayley asked.

"Yup. I need to fortify myself first." I gobbled a big bite of taco burger, four greasy french fries, and three huge gloppy spoonfuls of yogurt sundae. Then I stood up, balancing my tray. "Okay. Now I'm ready."

"Good luck," Hayley said, making sympathetic eyes.

Now I had to squeeze past Danny. "Bye," he grunted. I felt my cheeks burn. Brianna grinned, then waggled her fingers at me in a kind of Hollywood way. *What was THAT about?* I thought.

Fortunately, Mr. Mullaney's room was just down the hall from the lunchroom, so I didn't have far to carry my Mega-Lunch of Self-Pity. I bumped my tray into his door, causing Mr. Mullaney to look up from whatever unpublished "textbook" he was drooling over.

"Cassie," he remarked sarcastically.

I put my tray on my desk.

"We've already lost nine minutes," he complained. "Let's get to work. Start with number one on page one eighteen. Identify all relative clauses."

"Can I finish my lunch first, please?"

He made his lips into a straight line. If I'd had a protractor, I bet I would have measured a perfect one hundred eighty degrees. "Actually, Cassie, I'm doing you a favor by devoting this lunch period to review for tomorrow's quiz. Would you care to be prepared for it, or would you rather just continue daydreaming in class?"

"I wasn't daydreaming, I was writing! In my journal!"

Really, Cassie? Are you working on a story? Wonderful!

How exciting! Tell me all about it! I'm so glad you're immersed in the creation of literature: WHAT A DECENT ENGLISH TEACHER WOULD SAY.

INSTEAD, WHAT MR. MULLANEY SAID: "Page one hundred eighteen. Number one. Let's get cracking."

seven

"All right, then, Daeman, now aim for the red dot I painted in the center of the pillows," instructed Cat. She sighed. Why couldn't someone else, like Drael (Plaeth? Fraen? Kethael?), the Castle Archer, teach Daeman instead? She should be out there defending the throne from the Mystyck Beast and Valdyk's army, not sitting around the castle for hours on end, mindlessly teaching little Daeman how to aim at his stupid target.

Just then, Cat felt she was being watched. She looked up. The Queen's scheming Chief of Protocol, Sir Mullvo Clausebiter, was lurking by the feather pillows, with his customary sneer.

"Lady Catrain," he remarked sarcastically. "Whatever are you doing sitting there, mindlessly shooting at pillows? I thought you were out defending the realm!"

Cat looked up at him for just a moment. "I was," she said simply. "Now I'm not."

"Pity," Sir Mullvo sneered. "It seems like such a waste for a young lady with your famous Gift. Would you rather be doing something exciting and meaningful, or something totally boring and meaningless?"

"It's just temporary," Cat replied evenly, though she felt her cheeks becoming as fiery as her hair. "Now if you will excuse me, I have work to do."

"You certainly do," Sir Mullvo hissed as he practically slithered away. I hate him, I absolutely hate him, Cat thought.

Daeman watched Sir Mullvo exit the chamber. "Cat?" the little boy whispered. "Should you have spoken to him like that? Won't he get angry, and maybe even tell the Queen?"

"Don't you worry about him," Cat said.

"Let's just finish this target practice. Now watch closely as I aim for the center."

Cat carefully positioned the practice bow so that it was balanced just right in her arms.

Just then she heard Gloriana shreik (shriek?). "The Mystyck Beast! It's scorching the castle gate! Run!"

"Cassie? Can I tell you something?" Jackson was standing in the doorway of my room.

"Yeah, what?"

"What're you doing?"

"Homework!"

"Oh." Sniffle.

"You okay, Jackson?"

"Yeah. But the TV is making a funny noise and I can't get it to stop."

Oh, great. Just what I needed right now. "Define funny."

He shrugged. "Like it's buzzing. Like *bugs.* It did yesterday, but it stopped, but now it's not stopping."

I sighed. "Listen, Jackie, I'm too busy to deal with this right now. Go tell Miranda."

"I can't."

"Why not?"

"Because she left." Now Jackson came into my room, thrusting a note at me. "This was in the kitchen. Look."

Cass:
I'm at Madison's studying Chem for test tmrw. Be back at 6 (STILL YOUR TURN TO COOK!!!!!). Don't worry, I went shopping!!!!!

Be good,
Randa :)

P.S. If Adam Klein calls, PLEASE call me at Mad's: 555-0198. Thanx!!!!!

Great. So she was leaving me to babysit for Jackson until six, at which point I was supposed to cook supper. Wonderful, perfect, fabulous. I *hated* her.

Jackson sank down on my bed. He looked tiny all of a sudden. His blond hair stood up stiffly, like it hadn't been combed in a while. Come to think of it, when was the last time he'd had a decent shampoo? And why in the world was it *my* problem?

I dialed Madison's number. On the first ring, some girl answered. "'Lo," she said casually.

"Hello, this is Cassie Baldwin. Is my sister Miranda there, please?"

She must have handed the phone to Miranda, who must have been just sitting right there, probably waiting for this Adam person to call her.

"Yes?"

"First of all, Miranda, you could've *asked* if it was okay if you went to Madison's, instead of leaving me to babysit all afternoon."

"Who is this, please?" she asked pseudosweetly.

"You know exactly who this is. And what's wrong with the TV?"

"How should I know?"

"Jackson says it's buzzing. He says it sounds like it's full of bugs or something. *I* don't know. Did you notice anything yesterday?"

"Of course not. You think I have time to watch TV?"

"I think you have time for whatever you want, Miranda."

"Well, I don't. For your information I'm studying Chem, not TV repair, and I really can't chat with you on the phone right now."

"Yeah? Well, so sorry to disturb you."

"You're excused. Did Adam call?"

"Uh, no."

"Then, bye!" she said cheerily, and hung up.

Great. Just great. Now what was I supposed to do with Jackson until six o'clock if he couldn't even watch TV? I was *not* in the mood to play Power Rangers with him, that was for sure.

"So, Jackie boy," I said. "Would you like a snack, maybe?"

He nodded. *Well, that should kill some time,* I thought.

We went into the kitchen, where Mrs. Langley's care basket was still taking over the table. It was such a big basket that it seemed like a piece of furniture. We'd probably end up keeping it forever, always having to look at it to remind ourselves how "short of cash" we were. The milk and cream cheese were in the fridge, and the pastries were gone, but the apples, bananas, and oranges were all still there in the basket, looking suspiciously fresh, like poisoned fruit in a fairy tale.

I wouldn't eat any of it if you paid me.

But Jackson would. Anyway, it was different for him. "I want a banana," he announced.

"Please."

"Okay. Please."

I halfway peeled the banana, and then handed it to him.

"Thank you, Cassie," I reminded him.

He thrust out his lower lip. "Why do I have to say all that? You're not Mom."

"No, but I'm your evil omnivorous big sister, and I'll eat you if you're not polite!" I made my hands into claws and hovered over him like a raptor. Then I swooped down and started tickling his chest. But he just sat there, not giggling, not acting like a cute little brother.

I sighed. "Okay, Jackie boy, what's wrong?"

"My book report!" he blubbered.

Uh-oh. "That's right, you have a book report," I said. I once read somewhere that kids like to hear their negative feelings acknowledged, so I was "acknowledging" Jackson's.

It didn't work.

"When's Mommy coming home?" he wailed.

"Later. I'm not sure."

"Call her and ask!"

I hesitated. Mom kept telling us to call her at work "anytime," but she was hardly ever at her desk, and I felt funny about having her paged to ask her stupid stuff like, *Where did I put my library book? Can you check my Math homework?* So I hardly ever called, unless it was a total emergency. She would usually call us around five to "check in" and tell us she'd be missing supper, like it was late-breaking news. Of course she'd be missing supper; she always missed supper. Now it was only four fifteen. Could I stall Jackson for another forty-five minutes? Not likely. Besides, Miranda's not being here made this qualify as an emergency, didn't it?

I dialed Mom's number.

"Hello, this is Anne Baldwin. I'm not at my desk, but if you leave your name and number, I'll return your call. *Beeeeeeeep.*"

I hung up.

"Mom's on the phone, Jackie. She'll call us back in a few minutes."

"Call Mrs. Patella!"

"No way." We were supposed to knock on Mrs. Patella's door if there was a fire or a burglar or an earthquake or something, but the truth was, if there was any kind of real emergency, the *last* person I would ask to help was Mrs. Patella. All she seemed to do all day long was smoke cigarettes and panic. If she was waiting for a UPS delivery and it was a day late, she would knock on our door stinking of cigarettes and ask us a whole bunch of worried questions like, Were we here at three forty-five? Did we see the UPS truck go by? Were we sure it was the same driver? Were we sure we didn't receive it by mistake? Mrs. Patella was definitely a little crazy, but at least she didn't have Yorkies with bladder problems.

"But what if Mommy's working late again tonight?" Jackson demanded.

I groaned. "Jackie, listen. We'll do your book report, I promise. Just give me a minute while I call Miranda."

I dialed Madison's number again.

"'Lo," Madison repeated casually, like she was sitting by a pool.

"Hello, this is Cassie again. May I please speak to Miranda again?"

Miranda got on the phone, breathing loud. "He called?"

"What? Who?"

"Adam."

"No! *No!* Listen, Miranda, Jackson's really upset about this stupid book report thing. I tried calling Mom but she's not at her desk, and I don't know when she's coming home tonight, do you?"

Big dramatic sigh. "No, Cassie, I don't."

"Well, somebody's got to help Jackson. He's really upset."

Long pause. "Cassie, I told you I'm studying for this big Chem test tomorrow. Can't you just do it? It's a first-grade book report, how hard can it be?"

"It's not that it's hard, Miranda! I didn't say it was *hard.* But I feel like lately I'm doing everything around here, and I'm getting pretty sick of it. I mean, I have work too, you know!"

Another big sigh, but now a different tone of voice. Softer, more "reasonable." Ha! "Look, Cassie, I realize that I've been incredibly busy lately, but I'm in the middle of this huge academic crunch right now, and I really have to stay here and study. *Really.* Please, *please,* if there's any way you can just do this thing with Jackie today, I'll owe you big-time, I *promise.*"

What did I expect? That she was actually going to leave Madison's and the chance to sit on her butt and yak on the phone with this Adam person *if* he ever actually called? That she would come home to do a book report with her blubbering six-year-old brother who could barely even read a book, much less report on it? Yeah, right. That would, like, *so* happen.

By now it was pretty obvious I was dealing with one of those phony "choices," like the kind Mr. Mullaney was always giving us. Either

I. I could insist that she come home, which would either

A. not work, or

B. result in her actually coming home but being too attitudey to work with Jackson, who (whom?) I'd end up helping anyway;

OR

II. I could do the stupid book report with Jackson myself, and let her owe me "big-time," whatever that meant.

"Okay, Miranda," I said finally. "Okay. But this is the last time I'm letting you off the hook. I mean it. Starting tomorrow, you're staying here and watching Jackson like you *offered* to, or you are totally dead, I swear it."

"Deal," she said. "Okay, Cassie, gotta go now. You'll still call me if Adam calls, right?"

"Oh, sure, of course I'll interrupt your precious

'studying' to tell you something *so* incredibly important!" I slammed down the receiver. That was about the best I was going to do here, I realized.

I took a deep breath. "Okay, Jackie boy, now let's go get your book."

eight

Farmer Joe's Busy Week

Farmer Joe has a big farm.
He has pigs.
He has cows.
He has sheep.
He has a horse.
And he has a dog.
He feeds the pigs on Monday.
He milks the cows on Tuesday.
He shears the sheep on Wednesday.
He rides the horse on Thursday.
He walks his dog on Friday.
On Saturday he goes to town with his family. They go to the store.
What a busy week for Farmer Joe!

Great. Just monumentally great. "Jackie, what exactly is the assignment? Did Mrs. Rivera give you a sheet or something?"

He dragged his Spider-Man backpack into my bedroom, then handed me a crumpled sheet:

Book Report #3
Sometimes we want to change what we read. If you could change your book, what changes would you make? Be specific!

"Book report number three? You mean you've already done two of these?"

He shrugged. "Sort of."

"What does *that* mean?"

He shrugged again, his lower lip going into pout formation. I wasn't about to let him launch into full meltdown mode again if I could help it, so I quickly changed my approach.

"Okay, Mr. Baldwin. So, you've already read this thrilling bestseller, about to be made into a mooovie, get it?"

He chuckled, in spite of himself.

"So, let's quickly reread it, just to refresh our memory, okay?" I patted my bed, and he snuggled beside me, almost like a cat. Then I pointed to each word, and helped him read, slowly, sloooowly. He missed, like, ninety-eight percent of the words, no exaggeration. This shocked me. I mean, I knew he was having trouble with his reading, but I didn't know it was *that* bad. Then I wondered: Did Mom know about this? Did his teacher? And why was she giving him a stupid book report when the poor kid couldn't even get through this stupid book? I mean, if he couldn't read it, how was he supposed to "change" it?

"Okay, sir," I said, all businesslike. "Now, if you were turning this blockbuster novel into a major motion picture, what changes would you make?"

He shrugged. "Everything. I hate movies like that."

Movies like that? Name one. "Would you, um, make the book more exciting? Add a villain, or a tornado, or something?"

Shrug, head shake.

"Maybe a monster stomps all over the farm? Or a dinosaur?"

"Cassie, you know what? I don't think that's allowed."

"Listen, Jackie, just relax. I'll help you write this. You can write, can't you?"

"I guess."

What was his teacher doing all day? One thing I could say about Mr. Mullaney: At least he worked, even if everything he did was pointless and mind-numbing and evil.

"I have a question," I said. "Does Mrs. Rivera ever spend special time with you, to help you like this?"

"Not really."

"Never? She never sits down, just the two of you, and helps you sound words out or anything?"

"Maybe once. I don't remember." Big shrug up to his ears. The poor, poor kid. How could she just ignore him like that? Didn't she even care about him? Didn't she have any clue about what was going on in his life, how everybody (except me) kept abandoning him, flying off to Kraków, moving to Florida (maybe), leaving him behind to "study Chem" all the time? I was starting to get really angry now.

"Well, Jackie boy, I'll make sure Mrs. Rivera pays you some attention, don't you worry! Here's what we'll do. I'll tell you what to say, and you'll write the letters. You know your ABCs, right?"

Half-shrug. "Sort of."

Sort of? Things were definitely worse than I'd realized.

I wrote out the alphabet for him, nice and big, uppers and lowers. "Now I'll spell it out slowly, and you write the letters, okay?"

"Okay."

I dictated: *"My first thought was that* Farmer Joe's Busy Week *would benefit from the addition of conflict. For example, maybe a fire-breathing dragon could incinerate his crops. But then I realized: I didn't need to invent a villain. The story already had one: Farmer Joe himself! This guy is a total psycho! He feeds his pigs once a week, milks his cows once a week, walks his dog once a week, etc.??? If I could change anything about this book, I'd have Farmer Joe prosecuted for animal cruelty!"*

Jackson was clearly flagging in the writing department when the phone rang. It was Mom, "checking in," even though by now it was five forty-five.

"Sorry I couldn't call at five," she said breathlessly. "I was at a big crisis meeting."

"Another one?"

"Yes, another one. This place is nuts. Don't ever become a lawyer. Promise me, Cassie."

"I promise."

"Good. Everything okay?"

"Yup," I said. "I'm just finishing helping Jackson with his book report, and now I'm about to start supper. You sound like you'll be late tonight."

"Unfortunately, yes, sweetheart. Where's Miranda?"

"At Madison's. She'll be back any second."

"You mean she's been there the whole afternoon?"

"Oh, no," I said, then immediately kicked myself. Why in the world couldn't I just tell on Miranda? Was it to shield Miranda (who totally didn't deserve one ounce of my loyalty), or was it to shield Mom (who did)? Was I afraid Mom would just give up and rehire the strange women babysitters who made Jackson cry all the time? Or could there possibly be another reason I didn't even get myself?

"So, let me get this straight," Mom pressed on. "Miranda came home first?"

"Yeah," I said, pretty sure that was technically the truth. "But she forgot her Chem book, so she went to Madison's for a minute to borrow hers. She'll be right back."

"Hmmm. Really. Tell Miranda we'll be discussing this when I get home. Where's Jackie? Can you put him on?"

I handed the phone to my little brother, then went to the kitchen to start microwaving two frozen boxes. By the time Jackson hung up, the "suppers" were practically radioactive, and we ate them without talking, both of us wiped out from all that book reporting. Then we played Go Fish and I let the poor kid win, until Miranda finally walked in the door at seven twenty-five ("NO, HE DIDN'T CALL" is all I said to her). I gave Jackson a bath and a strawberry-and-banana-scented shampoo, got him into his Power Ranger pj's, and put him into bed. Then I stared at some Science for a quiz tomorrow, and then finally I got into my own bed, conveniently prewarmed by Buster and Fuzzy. It was only when I was 98 percent asleep that I realized I'd never had time to finish writing in my journal, but I figured, oh well, there'd be plenty of time for that tomorrow.

nine

Mr. Mullaney sneered. "Today, ladies and gentlemen, is a Double Day of Reckoning. Who knows why?"

"Quiz on relative pronouns?" guessed Zachary Hogan, this smirky little hairball, who was always either bragging about his test scores or sucking up to every single teacher we had.

"True, but why is it a Double Day?"

Silence.

"Isn't there something you're all forgetting?"

More silence.

"Should I just assume you're all unprepared, or should I give you the benefit of the doubt?"

Duh. Benefit. We want benefit!

"Cassie? Any ideas?"

Everyone turned to look at me, including Danny

Abbott. I felt my cheeks burn. *Journal,* Danny mouthed. He pantomimed writing. *Journal.*

I stared at him stupidly. Then I got it: Danny was trying to tell me that today was the first journal check. But that was impossible! I was positive the first journal check was next week, not this week! Could he be wrong? Could I be?

"Um, is it the first journal check?"

"Are you *asking* me, Cassie, or *telling* me?"

"Asking?"

"Wrong! You should be telling me." See? This man absolutely hated everything I ever said. "Yes, Cassie, it is the first journal check. Pass in your journals, everyone, and then we'll have our quiz. Let's get cracking!"

I took my journal out of my backpack and passed it in with the strong stomachachey feeling that I was dangerously underquota. We were supposed to write five single-spaced pages a week, and it was three weeks since this assignment started, so that meant fifteen pages. Had I written that much? When was the last time I'd counted? I couldn't even remember. Since I spent most of yesterday afternoon helping Jackie with his stupid book report about sadistic Farmer Joe, I'd hardly done any journal writing since class yesterday, which was when I got in trouble. Something told me I was a whole bunch of pages short. But the truth was, I was just so into the *story* that I wasn't really keeping track.

And then Mr. Mullaney passed out his Evil Quiz of Doom, so I couldn't waste any more time worrying about page numbers. Here is what we had to deal with:

Identify the Correct Relative Pronoun:

1. Scurvy was a disease (that, which) afflicted sailors (who, which, whom) suffered hideously from the deficiency of a nutrient (which, that) we call Vitamin C.

2. I read the will to Miss Von Faalkenburg, (whom, who) was benefited the least by the departed, (whose, who's) vicious joke left us all starving and penniless.

3. The man (who, whom) we called Uncle Bob confessed he'd been hiccupping nonstop since last April, a period (which, that) is roughly equivalent to seven dog years.

And so on. Whoa. Mr. Mullaney sure was a strange, strange man. I realized that if Danny hadn't bailed me out on the Double Day of Reckoning question, I'd probably be eating lunch with Mr. Mullaney until

Christmas. (*Which makes a better tree ornament, Cassie? Blinking lights or candy canes? Candy canes, you say? Are you ASKING me, or* telling *me?*). So at lunch, after filling my tray with neon-orange macaroni and cheese and another big gloppy yogurt sundae, I forced myself to sit next to Bess Waterbury. She was sitting catty-corner from Danny and, unfortunately, directly across from Zachary Hairball.

"That quiz was so easy it was a *joke*," he was practically shouting. "I can't believe Mullaney thought that was a *challenge*."

I gritted my teeth. Yeah, well, maybe not as big a challenge as digesting food across from *you*, you little oxymoron. I kind of leaned past Bess, which was not easy to do. "So, Danny, thanks for helping me out," I said.

He looked up, alarmed, then nodded.

"So, um, what did you get for scurvy?" I asked.

He looked even more alarmed. I realized that my question hadn't come out quite right, but it was too late to change it, so I just kept chattering on.

"And what was it? The repulsive pustule *which*, or the repulsive pustule *that*? And was it the sniveling toady *whom* or *who*?"

"Whom," Danny muttered, then quickly turned away.

Shhhhinguards! Could I have screwed that up any worse? Why couldn't I have just said thank you and left it at that? Now Danny probably thought I was as weird as Mr. Mullaney, and he'd never talk to me again. Plus, I was going to have to sit here for the rest of lunch listening to the Hairball shout about "jokes" and "challenges," and ignoring Bess Waterbury while she nibbled on her salad and tried to get me to talk to her. Suddenly that seemed unbearable. Totally, completely unbearable. Before I knew what I was doing, I picked up my tray and moved over to where Hayley and Brianna were sitting.

Brianna gave me a big smile. "So, Cassie. The wedding's off?"

"What?"

"We heard you and Danny called off the wedding," she explained. "Such a shame. You had the hall picked out and everything. And O-Bess would've made such a lovely maid of honor."

"If she could fit into the dress," Hayley said, giggling.

Now I glared at them both. "Shut up," I said.

Brianna smirked. "Oh, yeah, right. We forgot. Cassie Baldwin, Bess's personal bodyguard."

"And that's a lot of body to guard," said Hayley.

I felt my throat getting tight. "I'm not her bodyguard. I'm not even her friend. I can't help it if she keeps trying to talk to me!"

"So, go talk to her," said Brianna, nodding encouragingly. "Sit with her. I'm sure you two share a lot of interests."

"Well, we don't, Brianna. And for your information, she happens to be very nice. Why do you always have to make fun of her?"

"Why do *you* always have to act like you're better than everyone else?" Brianna shot back.

I was stunned. My mouth literally hung open. "What?" I repeated, like a moron.

"You heard me," said Brianna.

"But that's wrong, Brianna, I don't think—"

Then I just stopped. I wanted to defend myself, I wanted to tell them I didn't think I was better. I actually thought I was a totally excluded social zero who really just wished we could still go swimming together. But then I saw the way they exchanged a private look that meant something

I didn't understand—couldn't begin to understand—and suddenly I realized how badly I was doing these days. I was screwing up so many things in so many departments that it seemed impossible to keep track.

ten

Seventh period, the next-to-last class of the day, was Art. Art was actually sort of fun because the school had gotten a new kiln over the summer, so Ms. Sutter, our Art teacher, was always having us make sculptures. She didn't even care what we made, as long as she could bake it in the kiln. Once I made a six-headed Hydra, and she just said, "Very nice, Cassie," and snatched it from me and tossed it in to bake. But I never bothered to bring it home because a head came off.

Today, though, was too hot for the kiln. It was Indian summer, almost eighty degrees, and the sky was azure. *Azure. Azure. Azure. What a beautiful word,* I thought. It sounded like the name of a heroine. Maybe for my next novel, the one after Cat. *Lady Azure. Princess Azure. Azure, Queen of the Faeries.* So I wrote "azure" on a little slip of paper and stuck it in my jeans pocket.

Then I joined the rest of my Art class on the front lawn. Ms. Sutter was handing out sketch pads and number two pencils and putting a *shhh* finger over her mouth. "Listen carefully, everyone," she was saying. "We're going to try something a little different today. I'm going to break you up into groups of three, and you're going to wander around the front yard taking in this beautiful autumn day. Your group will choose something to sketch—maybe a tree, or a plant, or a rock, anything at all. Then you'll sketch it from three different angles. Any questions?"

Zachary Hairball's hand shot up. "Do we each sketch it from three different angles, or does each person in the group take a different angle?"

I was standing next to Danny, so I heard him groan.

"Each of you will take a different angle, because each of you approaches nature from your own special place," Ms. Sutter replied.

"And Zachary, your special place has bars," I muttered.

Danny guffawed, which made me feel proud, even though I'd just said a pretty mean thing.

But it was different from the stuff Brianna and Hayley said about Bess, I told myself.

Oh, really, Cassie? And why is that?

Because Zachary Hairball was always showing off and sucking up. But Bess was just trying to be friendly.

Oh. So it's okay to be mean to smirky little jerks?

Well, I wasn't mean *to* him; I was mean *about* him. And sometimes people just *deserve* meanness.

But not Bess. And of course not you.

Yup. That's exactly right. Not us.

While I was figuring all this out, Ms. Sutter was announcing that since Danny and I were the only ones left, we would have to be a group of two. And immediately we both started turning red because everyone else was in a group of three. But I guess it's not very surprising that Art teachers stink at division.

"Have fun, you guys," Brianna said, tittering. That made Danny walk ahead of me, even though we were supposed to pick the nature thing together.

Finally he stopped at a small red maple. "How about this?" he asked, like he just wanted to get it over with.

I shrugged. "Sure."

But actually I was glad. Because I'm the worst nature-sketcher in the world, but the one thing I can draw is trees. And the reason for that is, one day I read somewhere that when your IQ is being tested, a lot of the time the tester asks you to draw a man and a house and a tree. So I spent a lot of time practicing men standing in front of houses with trees. Just in case.

The only problem was, I only ever practiced one kind of tree, and it wasn't a red maple. But I knew that if I tried drawing a red maple, it would come out looking like a mushroom or a tube of toothpaste. So I automatically started drawing my standard sprawling sycamore.

Danny was standing on the other side of the red maple because he needed a different angle. That meant I couldn't see how his picture was coming out. But my guess was that it wasn't very good, because after he drew a few lines, he just tossed the sketch pad on the grass and plopped down.

"I hate Art," he grumbled. "I don't even see why we have to take it."

"What would you rather take?"

"Gym. Nothing but Gym."

"All day? Wouldn't that be incredibly boring?"

He scrunched up his face, and I thought, *Fabulous, Cassie. You practically just called him a potato.*

"I heard you like to swim," he said, picking up his pad again but avoiding eye contact.

"Yeah, I do. But I don't do it anymore."

"Why not?"

Why not? Well, that was a good question. Because we were practically destitute, and even if we *could* rejoin the fitness club, how would I get there and back three times a week? And even if I could work out transportation with someone *besides* Hayley and Brianna, who would watch Jackson?

And not just watch him, but actually take care of him. The truth was, I was really starting to worry about my little brother. Not only was he being ignored at school, where he wasn't even starting to learn to read, but he was also so teary and quiet at home. All he ever did lately was play Power Rangers in his room, but it was weird how you hardly ever heard a peep out of him. And he never asked to play with anyone from his class. That in a way was a relief, since the last thing I wanted was to have to deal with some other six-year-old boy after school.

Anyway, the point was, I couldn't just abandon Jackson three afternoons a week and go off swimming, even if by some miracle we could afford it and I could get a ride. But Danny didn't want to hear all that, and even if he did, I didn't want to explain it. To him or to anybody else, for that matter.

So all I said was, "I just don't."

"Too bad."

"I guess."

Think of something else, Cassie. Use syllables.

"Well, maybe all-day Gym wouldn't be so bad," I said. "At least there wouldn't be stupid quizzes about scurvy."

"Yeah," he agreed. "I hate English."

"I don't hate English, I just hate Mr. Mullaney. What is his *problem*?"

"Whatever it is, you'd better be careful," Danny said, now looking right at me. "He fails people all the time."

"Really? How do you know?"

"My brother had him two years ago. He had to repeat English in summer school. It totally wrecked our vacation."

I drew another branch on my sprawling sycamore, which was more and more resembling my semi-decapitated Hydra. "Well, fortunately, we don't have any vacation plans. And anyway, Mr. Mullaney would never fail *me. I'm* writing a novel."

And then I winced, because I realized I sounded exactly like Zachary Hogan.

eleven

Miranda shocked me by coming straight home from school that afternoon carrying two bulging bags of groceries.

"Well, lookee here," she announced. "Diet Coke, cat food, thank you, thank you, pasta, bread, peanut butter, tomato sauce, apples, lightbulbs, and yes, Ring Dings. No, please, hold your applause, you're too kind."

I had to smile. "Thanks, Miranda, really. But listen, can we talk about something?"

"Sure, sure. First I need to call Mad, then I have a U.S. History paper I need to finish up, then fine, no prob."

"Can't we talk now? It's important. About Jackie."

She stopped putting away the groceries to look at me. "What about him? He's okay?"

"Yeah, sure, he's *okay*."

Big dramatic sigh. "Listen, Cassie, I'll be happy to talk about SpongeBob, Britney Spears, anything you want, but *later*, like I said, all right?"

"Fine!"

The phone rang. Mom.

"Everything okay?"

Oh sure, Mom. Just peachy.

"Well, I'm about to step into a meeting. I may miss supper tonight, Cassie."

No problema. Have fun at your meeting. Later, Mom.

I grabbed a Ring Ding and sat down at my desk, which was so insanely cluttered with Post-its, eraser chunks, gum wrappers, pencil stubs, and wispy clouds of dustballs that there was barely room to work. Until Miranda was finally ready to squeeze in our little chat, what I really felt like doing was writing in my journal. I had this great idea about how Cat uses one of her dragonfire arrows to slay the Mystyck Beast, who *may* have killed the King. The King's exact whereabouts were still unknown, but maybe his army was just hiding in the woods somewhere, preparing an ambush. I didn't have all the details worked out yet, but it would be something really big and dramatic, that much I knew.

So I started hunting under the desk dirt for one of my black extra-fine-point Rolling Writers, or even, if absolutely necessary, a chewed-up pencil stub. But then my stomach clenched: Stupid me! Of course I couldn't write. Even now, my story was in the clutches of the evil Mr. Mullaney, who might be seriously unamused by his uncanny resemblance to Sir Mullvo Clausebiter. The thing was, I'd created Sir Mullvo after Mr. Mullaney had been so nasty to me at lunch. I *might* have erased him before the first journal check, which I thought was next week. Now, of course, it was too late. Would he penalize my grade for it? Would he make me stay in at lunch? If he was any kind of teacher, he'd be able to separate his own feelings (of embarrassment? betrayal? rage?) from his recognition of my talent. Okay, sure, my life was getting more chaotic and pathetic by the second. But I knew that my story was really, really good so far, way better than anything else I'd ever written. It may have been a page or two short, but so what? Even Mr. Mullaney would have to acknowledge how great it was, I told myself, despite how much he hated my guts.

The phone rang. So that meant Miranda was off the phone, finally—miracle of all miracles. I heard her say,

"No, sorry, who's calling?" then slam down the receiver. Guess it wasn't Adam. Poor Miranda, I thought, sitting by the phone, jumping every time it rang. No way was I ever going to turn into one of those pathetic teenage girls, so insanely desperate for a boy to call that it was like her whole life.

I started my Math homework, to get it out of the way. Dividing fractions: definitely a ten on the barf-o-meter. Mrs. Gillroy was a really nice Math teacher, kind of like a fat old grandmother who always made your favorite cookies when you came to visit. But she still couldn't get me to understand dividing fractions. I started the endless double-sided Math sheet; when I looked up, it was an hour later, and the phone was ringing again. "NO, SHE'S STILL NOT HERE," Miranda was saying over the "music" she listened to while "studying."

I got up from my desk and yelled down the hallway, "WHO WAS THAT ON THE PHONE, MIRANDA?"

"NO ONE!"

Now Jackson came out of his room looking flushed, probably from playing under the hot blanket. "Can I tell you something? I'm hungry," he announced.

Miranda finally turned off her "music" and joined us

in the hallway. "Okay, Jackie, but I'm just about to start supper, so no snacks."

"When will Mommy be home?"

"Later, so be a good boy and let me finish my history paper, and then I'll make you some yummy pasta, okay?" She scooped him up in her arms and twirled him around, kissing his cheeks. He yelped with joy, which should have made me happy, considering how miserable the poor kid seemed lately. Instead, for some strange reason, all I could say was, "Put him down, Randa, and stop treating him like a baby!"

She let him go, and he ran back into his room. I felt terrible. "What's your problem, Cassbrain?" Miranda accused.

"Nothing! It just really bothers me how you baby him all the time. He's not a baby, he's a person, and he's got problems too, just like the rest of us."

Miranda looked at me like I'd suddenly started speaking Icelandic. "What are you *talking* about?"

The phone rang again, and of course she immediately answered it. Apparently this time it was Madison Avenue, because she went into her bedroom and slammed the door. Every once in a while I could hear her screeching, "I DON'T BELIEEEEEVE IT!" When she came out twenty-five minutes later, she looked different. I couldn't figure it out, but it had something to do with her eyes.

"What's with your eyes?" I asked.

"You like? It's this new mascara, supposedly no-clump, but time will tell." She batted her eyelashes at me.

"You mean you were putting on makeup *while* you were talking on the phone just now?"

"Oh, really, Casshead, would you just please relax! This is what girls *do*, in case you haven't noticed lately."

"What's that supposed to mean?"

"Figure it out."

Then she flounced into the kitchen. I followed her, watching as she started boiling water, presumably for Jackson's pasta. We didn't have any butter, which he absolutely had to have on his "squiggles," but after she'd just insulted me like that, I was too stunned to say anything. And anyway, it was fine with me if Miranda had to deal with one of his meltdowns for once.

"So, about Jackie. What's going on?" she asked, gritting her teeth as she opened the jar of tomato sauce.

The phone rang again. "Shoot!" she shouted. Then she picked up the receiver. "NO, SHE ISN'T, SORRY!" She slammed the receiver down.

"Telemarketer?"

"No, some psycho named Pauletta Rivera who keeps calling and calling to talk to Mom."

Pauletta Rivera? As in Mrs. Rivera?

"Uh, Randa, I don't think you should have done that just now," I said slowly. "I think that was Jackson's teacher you just hung up on."

"Really?" She blinked her no-clump eyes. "Well, why didn't she say so? Jackson, get over here!"

Jackson walked into the kitchen like he was afraid of getting yelled at, which was a pretty good guess.

"Were you naughty at school today?" Miranda asked.

"Noooo," he said, looking at his feet.

"You sure?"

"Morgan said I pushed him on the swing, but I told Mrs. Rivera I didn't."

"You didn't push him, or you *told* Mrs. Rivera you didn't?"

Clearly he didn't get the difference. "I told Mrs. Rivera I didn't push him, but she didn't believe me," he announced.

Then he burst into tears. Way to go, Miranda.

Even she seemed surprised by his reaction. She gave him a big long hug, like he was her favorite stuffed animal.

Then she sat him, still hiccupping, in front of whatever was on Cartoon Network. From the kitchen I could hear that the TV was buzzing, just like Jackson had said it was.

"I can't watch this," I heard him say. "It's broken (hic)."

"Well, read a book, then," Miranda snapped, her patience clearly over. "I'm not Mr. Fix-It, you know!"

She stormed back to the kitchen, shaking her head. "What's the deal with Jackie?"

So, finally I had her attention. "Listen, Miranda, I don't know, but I seriously think Jackie may have some sort of learning disability or something."

"Whoa," she said. "What makes you think that?"

Then I told her about sadistic Farmer Joe, and how Jackson hardly even knew the alphabet, and how teary he's been after school, which, of course she didn't know about because she was never here, or if she was here, she was in her room putting on mascara and yakking to Madison or dreaming about this Adam person or listening to "music." Except I left all that last part out, because I was too tired for all-out war.

She listened quietly, like she was finally getting it. Then she heaved one of her world-famous big dramatic sighs. "Cassandra," she said.

"What?"

"Don't take this the wrong way, but I really, really think you're making way too much of this. Jackie is just a little boy who misses his mommy, his nanny, and guess what, maybe even his daddy. That's why he cries all the time, not because of Farmer Joe. And if he's having trouble reading, he's supposed to be. He's only in first grade, remember?"

"Of course I remember! But after spending all that time working with him on his stupid book report, I also think he may have some sort of reading problem!"

"Cassie, my love, I think *you* have some sort of *life* problem, in the sense that you need to *get* one."

Then she sprang up. "Whoops! The pasta!" she cried. She drained it frantically, scrunching up her face in the cloud of steam.

I watched her, but I wasn't going to help. I wasn't finished talking. Besides, the way she kept running out on me, locking herself in her room to "study," wasting all that time at Madison's house, this might be my only chance. "Randa?"

"Yup?"

"I have a public service announcement for you: All

girls don't wear mascara. You don't have to wear mascara to be a girl!"

"Oh, come on, Cassie. That's not what I said."

"And for your information I have a life! A *twelve-year-old* life."

"Well, good for you, Casshead. Congratulations. Now let's just get supper on the table, okay?"

I stared at her, amazed. "Get it yourself, Miranda," I said.

Then I stomped back to my bedroom and slammed the door.

twelve

I sat at my desk for the next half hour, writing a list of all the insulting adjectives I didn't call Miranda to her face:

Insipid
Trivial
Superficial
Vapid
Girly-girly
Egotistical
Shallow
Hopeless
Barfheaded
Potatobrained
Vain

These were all new additions, joining the long list of other Miranda-related adjectives, such as "selfish," "lazy," and "irresponsible." Don't get me wrong, Miranda was definitely still selfish, lazy, and irresponsible. Incredibly, as a matter of fact. But after that crack about the mascara, I was starting to see her in a completely different way. Now, in addition to blowing off Jackson and sucking up to Mom and forgetting to shop for the basic necessities of human life, she seemed to be the complete and total President of the Club for Girls Who Think About Nothing All Day Long Except Their Own Meaningless Appearances.

Whereas I thought about literature. And writing. And books. And words in general, especially cool words, like "vapid" and "insipid."

Plus, I also thought about people's feelings, which Miranda clearly didn't have a clue about. She didn't care about Jackson, and she certainly didn't care about me. Because if she did, even the tiniest fraction of an iota, she never would have said such a vicious thing.

This is what girls do, in case you haven't noticed lately.

What in the world was that supposed to mean? That I didn't know how to be a girl, just because I used my *brain* instead of my *face*? Or that lately I've been so busy taking care of everything and everybody that I've forgotten how to *be* a girl?

Well, even if that was true, whose fault was that?

I don't think I'd ever been so angry in my whole life.

I was so angry that even listing insulting adjectives wasn't calming me down. And when I heard a knock on my closed door, I just shouted, "GO AWAY!"

But the door opened anyway, and in walked Miranda.

"You're in my room," I growled.

"Well, duh," she said. Then she sat down on my bed, startling Buster, who jumped off on principle. "Listen, Cassie, I'm really sorry. I said a stupid, nasty thing before, and I didn't mean it."

"Ha!"

"But I didn't. I was just so stressed out with the phone ringing and Jackie crying, and having to make supper. Then you made that big speech about learning disabilities, which I totally disagree with, by the way. Anyway, I took it all out on you, and I'm very, very sorry."

I stared at her, shocked. This was maybe the first real, totally sincere, from-the-bottom-of-her-heart apology Miranda had ever given me. I mean, ever, in her whole life. Her eyes were so serious that I had to smile.

"Well, okay."

She grinned back, looking incredibly relieved. "So, are you hungry, Casshead? There's still some pasta left, if you want."

Actually, I'd forgotten all about supper. It's funny how sometimes food is so important, more important than anything else in the universe, and other times it's the last thing on your mind.

"Maybe later," I said. "Where's Jackie?"

"In his room putting on pj's. I just finished giving him his bath. That kid was *filthy*."

"I know. We need more of that strawberry shampoo he likes."

"I'll make a list. So, what do you say? Wanna watch some TV or something?"

"We can't," I said. "It buzzes, remember?"

She rolled her eyes. "Oh, yeah, right. Too bad Dad's not around. He could fix anything."

"He could?"

"Of course! You don't remember? Well, yeah, I guess you were really little that time you broke the washing machine."

"I what?"

"Yeah, you clogged it up with some rocks. They fell out of your pocket, I think. Anyway, Dad fixed it. He was really proud of himself. And remember that old computer?"

"No. What old computer?"

"This huge enormous piece of junk they didn't want at his office? Maybe four or five years ago?"

I shook my head.

"Well, Dad lugged it home and fixed it. It took him, like, two weeks, but he did it. Then Mom ordered a pizza to celebrate."

"It's amazing that I don't remember that," I said, wondering.

"Yeah, well, you were younger. And I guess you don't notice everything when it's happening. You just assume it's the way things *are*." She stood up then, which clearly meant the subject of Dad was over. "So, come on, Cassie. Wanna do some stupid girl stuff?"

"Like what?"

"I don't know. Like polishing our toenails. Or looking at fashion mags. Or checking out Mom's perfumes."

"You're kidding, Miranda, right?"

"And we can eat frozen Ring Dings," she continued,

grinning mischievously. “I threw them in the freezer. They’re probably not totally solid yet, but I tried them at Mad’s house and they’re the *best!*”

I started giggling. “And we can wear fuzzy slippers and give each other new hairstyles, and you can tell my fortune.”

“That’s right,” she nodded, happy that I was playing the game. “And then we’ll read each other’s diaries, and you can tell me all about the boy you secretly like.”

“Whoa,” I said. “Stop right there!”

She batted her no-clump eyelashes. “But why, Cassandra? Did I say something wrong?”

I laughed. “Never mind. How about if we just eat frozen Ring Dings instead?”

“You’re on,” she said, and we went into the kitchen.

thirteen

Third period the next day, Mr. Mullaney handed back the journals. Normally when teachers hand back tests and quizzes and the stupid, mindless homework they even bother to collect, I just glance at the grade ultracasually, as a kind of anti-Smirky Hairball policy. But this time I immediately flipped to the last page of my Cat story, where Mr. Mullaney had written something in spidery black ink in the middle of the margin: "12".

Right after my last paragraph, the one where the Mystyck Beast is attacking the castle.

"12".

Not: "Great start, Cassie!"

Or: "I love your dialogue!"

Or: "You've created some excellent characters! Cat is cool!"

Or: "Great action scenes! I love the way you build suspense!"

Not even: "I can't wait to read the next installment!"

Just: "12".

Twelve! For about two and a half seconds I thought maybe it was twelve on a scale of one to ten, like it was so great it was just off the charts, you know, an A plus-plus. But then Mr. Mullaney announced that Zachary Hairball got the highest grade, because *he* turned in twenty-six pages. Whereas I, who was working on a whole *novel*, got a puny, pathetic *twelve* because I was short three pages. And of course, page count was all that mattered, as far as Mr. Mullaney was concerned.

"Um, excuse me, Mr. Mullaney, but I was wondering if you really read my story," I said to him after class was over, my voice coming out kind of strangled.

He gave me an icy look. "What's the question here, Cassie? Whether or not I did my job, or whether or not you did yours?"

And that's all he would say. He started stacking some loose papers from his stupid "fiction textbook," not looking at me, clearly wanting me to leave. So I left. I was *furious*. After I spent all that time worrying that he would be offended by Sir Mullvo Clausebiter, he didn't even bother to read my stupid journal, he just counted the stupid pages! Why had I even bothered to do it? Why had I taken it so seriously? Why had I stayed up so late, sitting at my desk, trying to make it as perfect as possible?

I was still steaming when I sat down at lunch.

"Can you believe that?" I demanded. "He just counted the pages, he didn't even read what I wrote!"

Brianna rolled her eyes. "Yeah, well, what did you expect, Cassie? Like he's going to start respecting us all of a sudden?"

"Well, I worked really hard on this story I'm writing," I said. "It's maybe the best thing I've ever written, and he didn't even look at it!"

She snorted. "So? He did that to all of us, not just to *you*, Cassie."

Then Danny, who happened to be sitting at our table, said, "You should do what I do."

I stared at him. After my Zachary Hairball imitation that day we were sketching trees, I didn't expect he'd ever talk to me again, and here he was offering advice.

"All I did was write some top-ten lists, you know, Top Ten Video Games, Top Ten Movies, Top Ten TV Shows,

Top Ten Basketball Players, Top Ten Baseball Players—"

"We get it," Hayley, said, laughing.

"Okay. Then I just explained why they made the list. Like, for Top Ten Movies, I wrote, 'Great car chase' or 'Great special effects,' something like that."

"That was smart," I said. "You probably didn't work very hard."

Shut up, Cassie! I yelled at myself. *What a completely dorkheaded thing to say!*

But Danny shrugged, like I'd paid him a compliment. "Yeah, thanks," he said.

"I just wrote summaries of books I like," Hayley said. "Lots of details. And I wrote really big, and had really big margins. He didn't mind—I got a fifteen."

Bess Waterbury was sitting by herself at the next table over, but now even she joined in. "I wrote nineteen haikus," she said.

"One to a page?" I sputtered. "He COUNTED that?"

She nodded. "Yeah. I mean, I worked kind of hard on them, but they're only three lines each."

I groaned. *Shhhipwreck.* Stupid, stupid, stupid me.

"And what were they about, Bess?" Brianna asked, in this kindergarten teacher sort of voice.

"What difference does it make?" I snapped. "That's not even the point."

"Well, maybe you don't care about Bess's hard work, but we do," said Hayley. "Tell us all about your haikus, Bess."

"Don't, Bess," I said.

"Don't worry, Cassie, I wasn't going to," she answered, but her voice had a funny catch.

"Oh no, now Bess is upset," Hayley announced. "And we were just trying to include her in the conversation."

"Yeah, right," I said.

"Of course we were. What were we doing, then?" She raised her eyebrows first at me, then at Brianna.

Brianna shook her head. "Cassie doesn't believe us," she informed Hayley.

"I know," Hayley agreed, nodding. "That really, really hurts my feelings, Cassie."

I gave them my evilest glare. "Just stuff it, both of you, okay? *Okay?*"

Brianna sighed. "Well, Cassie, if you absolutely refuse to believe us, why don't you just get up and go over to Bess. You can sit there for the rest of lunch and comfort her."

"Maybe I will!"

"Okay, that's it, I'm out of here," Danny muttered. We watched him cram his Styrofoam tray into the trash, then shove open the door with his shoulder as he left the cafeteria.

"Oops," said Brianna. "I think you scared him away. Nice going, Cassie."

"Just. Shut. Up," I hissed.

"Aren't you going to run after him?"

I didn't even bother to answer that, because it wasn't close to an actual question. Anyway, pretty soon Brianna and Hayley started talking about some swim team thing, which was a way of announcing that as far as they were concerned I was officially invisible. For an iota of a second I actually did consider switching tables to sit with Bess. Then I decided, no, that would just be a formal declaration of war, and I wasn't in the mood.

Besides, I had something else to think about. Something way, way, *way* more important. Namely this: Here I'd been all worried that Jackson had a learning disability, when it turned out that I, Cassandra Baldwin, was the one with a complete and total *school* disability. After eight grades (counting kindergarten) I didn't know the first thing about getting good grades with the least amount of effort possible, which was clearly something everyone else was mastering big-time. Instead of watching TV or reading or riding my bike or doing something meaningful, I was spending my entire free time writing this whole fantasy *saga.* I was thinking about the characters all day long as if they were real people, planning plot twists, imagining costumes and castles and horses and swordfights, hearing dialogue in my head as if I were watching a really good movie. Cat was real to me—better than real. More important than real. Her story—my story about her, I mean—was the biggest, best thing in my life these days. Meanwhile, everybody else in my class was treating this journal thing as if it were a big fat, stupid joke. And guess what: The joke was really on me, because I cared so much that I missed the whole point of the assignment, which was that it *had* no point. Top-ten lists? Book summaries? Haikus? Big margins? Maybe Miranda was right. Maybe, for once in her life, my sister was actually right about something.

Maybe I really did need to get a life.

fourteen

From then on I decided not to care. If everyone else was writing totally pointless garbage in their journals and getting away with it—getting *praised* for it—then that was exactly what I was going to do. Why share my story—which was something really precious, which was so-called fantasy, but also, in some weird way, FACT, with this mindless, sadistic teacher who was just going to count the stupid number of pages? If all he wanted us to do was fill pages, fine, I'd fill pages. I'd give him exactly what he wanted, and I'd get an A. And I'd have a life. Maybe not a Miranda-life (yakking to Madison Avenue, dreaming about this Adam person, blah blah blah), but better than that. Well, if not exactly better, at least my own.

So, when I got home from school that day, I went

straight to my desk. I opened my regulation two-hundred-page college-lined spiral notebook, uncapped my black extra-fine-point Rolling Writer, and got to work:

Top Ten Stupidest Things Miranda Ever Said

1—Omigod!

2—Oh. My. God.

3—This is what girls do—

Then I stopped. No. However stupid this journal was going to be from now on, it was mine, not Miranda's. Let her fill up her own stupid journal with her own stupid words. I tore out the page and tossed it into my overflowing garbage can. Then I stared at my insanely messy desk. Suddenly I had an idea. I'd use the garbage on my desk for inspiration. Garbage to create garbage.

A Virtual Tour of My Insanely Messy Desk

When you want to write, it's important to have a clean desk. So first, throw out all the random thingies on your workspace. This includes: old gum wrappers, dustballs, leaky pens, dried-up markers, pencils that are too short, pencils that have dirty erasers, pencils that have no erasers, old Post-its that don't stick, old Post-its that have writing, old Post-its in weird colors, reinforcements (because who actually uses them?), rulers (because ditto), rubber bands (distracting), dirty tissues (disgusting), staplers (dangerous). Also throw out calendars. Calendars on your desk just add pressure, and who needs that?

I read over my work. Perfect. It took me exactly two and a half minutes to write this no-brain garbage, and with my newly big handwriting, I'd already filled almost half a page. Yessir, I thought. I was definitely getting the hang of it.

I went into the kitchen. The refrigerator hummed. I opened it: empty as usual. This morning Mom had written out a shopping list for Miranda, who, guess what, was late again. *Fine,* I thought, *great. Thank you, Miranda Baldwin.* I went back to my room, got my journal, brought it to the kitchen, reopened the refrigerator, and wrote:

A Virtual Tour of My Empty Refrigerator

Due to circumstances beyond my control, namely my hopeless, irresponsible, selfish big sister, our refrigerator is empty. Well, not exactly empty. We do have:

1. Spicy brown mustard,
2. Honey mustard,
3. Tarragon mustard,
4. Weird green cat-barf-looking mustard,
5. Country mustard (in what sense? Is it from this country? Does it taste like the country? A scary thought!),
6. Dijon mustard (what does that mean? Do they eat a lot of mustard in Dijon? If so, why?),
7. A charity orange,
8. Five apples (one charity),
9. A half-gone pint of charity cream cheese,
10. A half-gone gallon of charity milk,
11. An open can of Friskies Turkey & Giblets (What exactly are giblets? They sound kind of cute!),
12. And a half-gone liter of Diet Coke.

Maybe not the best-stocked refrigerator in Emerson, but hey. At least there's no tofu!

Just then, Fuzzy jumped into my lap. He only did that when he wanted to be fed, or stroked, or complimented, which was always. So I rubbed my face in his warm fur and told him he was a good boy, a great boy, a beautiful boy. This gave me an idea. Another virtual tour? Well, maybe not.

Cats Rule, Dogs Drool

Cats are great. Some people prefer dogs, but what do they know? Cats are better in every way. First of all, cats purr, which is a great sound to hear when you're feeling psycho. Also, purring puts you to sleep, which is helpful when you're up late at night stressing out about some stupid, mindless, pointless assignment for school. (Like what, I wonder?) Cats also prewarm your bed, which is better than using an electric blanket, because cats have rarely been known to electrocute anyone. They chase dustballs under *the bed, which means you don't have to bother vacuuming. (Not that you would.) And they groom themselves just for fun, which is always amusing. Of course, when my sister grooms herself just for fun, it's stupid and pathetic, but that's another story.*

The phone rang. "Hello, this is Pauletta Rivera, may I speak to Anne Baldwin, please?"

Jackson's teacher! "I'm sorry, she's not available right now," I recited, just like Mom taught us to say when she was at work. But then I had a thought. "This is Cassie Baldwin. Jackson's sister. How are you?"

"Fine, thanks," Mrs. Rivera said, sounding surprised. "And you?"

"Great. Actually, Mrs. Rivera, my mother did mention that she wanted to speak with you. Something about Jackson's reading, I don't remember what, exactly. Something about how concerned she was that maybe Jackson had a learning disability or something. I think she said she wanted to have him tested."

"Oh! Really!" she said. "Well, I should certainly speak to her, then. What time will she be home?"

Later. "Any minute, but would you like to try her at work? I can give you her work number."

"Thank you, but I already have it. I'll just call her there, since this is important." Mrs. Rivera thanked me, and then I speed-dialed Mom to warn her, but I just got her voice mail. So would Mrs. Rivera, I thought, but at least it was a start.

The door opened. I could hear Miranda and someone else.

"CASSIE? YOU HOME?"

I raced to my desk. "JUST DOING HOMEWORK!" I yelled down the hall.

Cats zoom around the house for no reason, which is always good for a laugh.

She popped her head into my doorway. "Hey, Casshead, I want you to meet my darling amiga, Madison."

She shoved Madison Avenue into my room. Madison was wearing a black warm-up jacket that made her look sort of athletic, except her hair had streaky blond highlights and she stank like perfume.

"HI!" she exclaimed, then ran out, giggling. "Why did you DO that?" she shrieked at my sister.

I liked her already.

Also, cats are conveniently droppable on your sister's head.

I heard them banging doors in the kitchen. "CASSIE, WHERE'S ALL THE RING DINGS?" Miranda shouted down the hall.

"WE ATE THEM LAST NIGHT, REMEMBER?"

"ALL OF THEM?"

"YUP."

Loud foraging.

Cats are (mostly) quiet.

"WHY IS THERE NEVER ANYTHING TO EAT IN THIS HOUSE?"

Uh, Miranda? Is this, like, Rhetorical Questions for Dummies or something? If I answer it, will you tell me to get a life, or chill out, or something equally stupid and insulting?

They are sensitive to your needs.

"MAYBE YOU SHOULD DO THE SHOPPING!"

"YEAH, MAYBE! LISTEN, WE'RE GOING TO MAD'S. YOUR TURN TO COOK SUPPER, CASS!"

"GREAT! OKAY, THEN, BYE!"

Cats keep you company.

The front door slammed. It wasn't until they were gone that I realized she hadn't even checked in on Jackson. Wonderful, I thought. Here she was acting like I was this no-life loser who didn't know a single thing about my little brother while she was the one who understood him so incredibly well. But she didn't even bother knocking on his door before she went over to Madison's to sit by the phone and stuff her face with Ring Dings. She might as well have been going to Kraków or Florida or *Mount Doom* for all the attention she was paying! So I got up from my desk, went into Jackson's room, and crawled under his blanket, where the air was hot and slightly farty, and Jackson and I played Power Rangers until it was time for me to nuke something for dinner.

fifteen

Mr. Mullaney spent the whole period going over his insanely evil grammar quiz, but what did I care? I got a 68, the worst grade I'd ever gotten in English in my whole life, but so what? *So what?* I just kept writing in my journal the whole stupid period, filling up page after page after page:

The Many Uses of Rubber Bands

Rubber bands are very useful. They make excellent "worms" for psycho cats. They're also necessary for slingshotting Chiclets across the room. You can chew on rubber bands if you want some no-carb chewing gum (no cavities, too!). They make great doorknob decorators. You can twang them in your mouth, if you wear braces. You can snap them on people's knees when you want to annoy them. Rubber bands also make great fidget toys during Math, when the teacher is telling you how to divide fractions for the ten millionth time, and you're not allowed to scream. They make delightful go-with-everything bracelets for the fashion-impaired. And they're always useful for holding your shoes together, if you're short of cash.

I crossed out that last bit—none of Sir Mullvo's business. But those three nasty words, "short of cash," reminded me that I'd never sent a thank-you to Mrs. Langley. Fine. No problem. I'd do it now.

Dear Mrs. Langley,

Thank you for the lovely gift basket. It was so nice of you to give us those delicious treats! We really enjoyed them all. Hope to see you soon.

Love,
The Baldwin family

Dear Mrs. Langley,

Thank you for the care package. It was incredibly tactless of you to remind us that we're "short of cash." In case you were wondering, we practically choked on the "scrumptious" blueberry muffins. Does this make you feel superior?

Ungratefully,
The Baldwin family

Yo, Jojo,

Just because you let your two stupid dogs pee on our grass (when we had grass), does this make you think you need to feed us? Next time, just buy your stupid dogs some diapers and skip the muffins. We'll be fine.

Don't write back,
What's left of
The Baldwin family

"Cassie?"

"Yes?"

"I'll ask again: Is the correct answer 'the slobbering ogress *who*,' or 'the slobbering ogress *whom*'?"

"Whom?" I guessed.

Dead silence. Then I could hear Brianna giggling.

"Wrong," Mr. Mullaney sneered.

"Oh, right! Who?"

"Wrong again."

"What? How can they *both* be wrong?" I spluttered.

"They can both be wrong, Cassie, because there *is* no ogress, slobbering or otherwise. I just threw that at you to see if you were paying attention. Which clearly you were not."

Then Zachary Hogan, the smirky little hairball, raised his hand. "Mr. Mullaney, isn't 'which clearly you were not' a sentence fragment?"

"Yes, of course, Zachary. Excellent."

Zachary beamed.

Mr. Mullaney didn't beam. He looked at me like he was pointing a dragonfire arrow.

"Therefore, Cassie, I am issuing a warning. One more episode of inattentiveness, one more unauthorized trip to fantasyland, and I will need to contact your parents."

"Good luck," I muttered.

sixteen

There's an art to lunchroom dining. You fill your tray (today, chicken nuggets, fries, gloppy yogurt), then process your card (now mine was under by sixteen dollars and seventy cents; but you can't seem alarmed, you have to act like, whoops, you just keep forgetting to tell your parents), then scan the lunchroom for a place to sit. But you can't stand there looking for too long or else everyone will think you're a freakish loser with zero social options. So you zoom in to spot your "friends," the guaranteed few who'll save you a seat. Even if you hate them. Even if they hate you back.

So I did, and of course, they didn't. Save me a seat, that is. Brianna and Hayley were sitting at the table closest to the water fountain, with Zachary Hogan, the smirky little hairball, and Lindsay Frost, this snotfaced girl from swim team. Lindsay was leaning across the table to tell them something obviously private, and they were all laughing like whatever she said was so incredibly amusing. And it was really obvious, even from a distance, that there was absolutely no room at that table for me.

Crappachino. Turd, turd, turd. Yeah, okay, but what was I expecting? Hayley and Brianna were in their own private little world of whispers and giggles. Apparently they opened it up to let in Lindsay, but that wasn't exactly surprising. Lindsay swam with them at the fitness club every Tuesday, Thursday, and Saturday, so of course they shared blow-dryers and towels. And secrets, too, probably. More than probably: definitely. I could see it by the way their dark-blond heads came together. They were a group, a trio. I really didn't like Lindsay *at all.* She flipped her hair all the time and wore this pink lip-gloss that made her mouth look all sticky, like she ate too much cotton candy for breakfast or something. She always flirted with these total jerks on the boys' swim team, like Mike Greenwall and Ryan Francona, who wouldn't know what to do with a book if they sat on one. And to me she always acted all condescending. (When I quit the swim team—that is, had to quit—she touched my arm and said, "I heard the news—

I just feel *awful* for you, Cassie," like I had a brain tumor or something). So, actually I wouldn't want to sit there even if they had saved me a seat. Which, of course, they hadn't.

Okay, fine, I get it, I thought. So on to Plan B. But what was Plan B? The thing about seventh grade is that all the groups are totally set. Starting in fifth grade, you figure out your group to eat with, hang out with at recess, even hang out with on weekends (although the truth is, I hadn't done that in a long, long time). Even if you hated every single kid in your group, even if they bored you/ignored you/insulted you/disgusted you, it was still your group. All things considered, you were lucky to have it.

But what if somehow, in some weird way you couldn't quite figure out, your group gradually stopped being your group? It's not like you could just bring your lunch tray over to some other table—say, the Jock table, or the Dork table, or the Video Game table. It's not that they would actually *prevent* you from sitting with them. It's just that they would totally ignore you and make you feel like a big wet puddle of cat barf. So you were better off, much better off, sitting by yourself, or else sitting with some other groupless loser, and praying that lunch would end quickly. Like in a zillionth of a nanosecond.

So there I was with my tray, scanning the lunchroom for some place, any place, to sit down *fast* before the whole seventh grade could tell that I'd lost my group. I could've sat down next to Katie Chang, who was kind of boring but otherwise okay, but she was sitting with this girl actually named India. The two of them were definitely another best-friends unit, though, and I decided I just couldn't deal with any more of *that.* I also vetoed sitting with Mariah Silverman (because all she talked about was MTV), Arianna DeVito (because all she talked about was grades), and Tara Nolan (because all she talked about was Tara Nolan).

Right next to the Video Game table were Danny Abbott and his best friend, Noah Davis. There was definitely enough space for me to squeeze in there, I thought. But did I want to? Well, of course I wanted to, but would I actually do it? It was one thing if I was sitting with Brianna and Hayley and then somehow we ended up talking to Danny. It was completely different to actually walk up to his table *on my own* and just *sit down.* And he was with Noah. Maybe if he'd been sitting there all by himself, maybe then *possibly* I'd have gone over and sat down with him. But under these circumstances how could I walk over there and interrupt whatever conversation they were having and just start talking to him like, ho hum, isn't that Mr. Mullaney such a bore?

I stood there in front of the lunchroom balancing my tray full of chicken nuggets, and then suddenly it hit me: I WAS SOUNDING EXACTLY LIKE MIRANDA.

I was. I really was. I was turning into everything I despised: a girly-girly, squealing, yakking, Adam-waiting, *pathetic loser.* Just like Miranda. Just like her trusty sidekick, Madison Avenue.

I felt like barfing. And of course Danny picked that moment to look across the lunchroom *right at me.*

So I looked down at my tray like, what do you know? Chicken nuggets! How'd they get here?

And then I sat down with Bess Waterbury.

Today she was eating a blob of cottage cheese and some fruit salad that looked like it was preserved in formaldehyde. Probably tasted that way too.

"Okay if I sit down?" I asked, sitting down.

She stared. "Sure."

I started eating my chicken nuggets, which by now were so cold they tasted like chicken rocks. She watched me.

"Want a bite?" I asked.

"Yeah, but I can't. I'm on this diet. I'm trying to lose, like, fifty pounds."

"Wow," I said, chewing. "That's a lot."

"Yup. I've already lost six. But you know my whole family is fat. We have a genetic predisposition. It's weird how things run in families."

Now it was my turn to stare. After realizing I'd just been having a Miranda Moment, this wasn't what I wanted to hear. I quickly changed the subject.

"So, Bess, have you written any more haikus lately?"

She shook her head. "No, I'm tired of those. Now I'm writing a story. Well, actually, it's kind of long, so maybe it's more of a novel. How's yours going?"

I winced. "I gave it up."

"Really? Why?"

"Why not?"

"Because. You said it was the best thing you ever wrote."

I felt like I'd been slapped. "Yeah, well, it was," I said, "and that jerk Mr. Mullaney doesn't deserve it! I mean, I worked so hard on it, I cared about it so much, and he made me feel like it was garbage. It's like I was, I don't know, sharing something precious, like a gift, and he was treating it like it was nothing."

She poked at her cottage cheese blob for a while. Then she said, so quietly I could barely hear, "Yeah. But if you stop writing it, then he won."

I swallowed. My throat felt tight, and it wasn't from the rocky chicken, either.

"So," she said, finally. "What was it about?"

"Nothing. I don't know. It was this sort of fantasy adventure story."

Now she grinned. "I love those! It's all I read."

"Really?"

"Yeah! I've read every single Tamora Pierce. And Robin McKinley and Nancy Springer. She's my favorite. Have you read *I Am Morgan le Fay*?"

I grinned back. "Only, like, six times."

Bess actually laughed. "My mom hates them. She says they're all the same."

"No, they aren't! Not the good ones!"

"That's what I told her, but she doesn't believe me. Now she won't let me buy any more until I get rid of my old ones."

"You have a lot?"

"Millions. Maybe I can give you some? If you like."

I looked at her hard. Was she wrapping up some

"charity novels" in dorky pink cellophane because she'd heard somewhere that I was "short of books"? But Bess was looking right back at me, with a kind of question in her eyes. No, I decided, she wasn't embarrassed or pseudosympathetic or anything. And her eyebrows were up, like she was really hoping I'd accept. "Sure," I said. "That would be great. Thanks."

Then we pretended to eat our lunches. By now my yogurt sundae was beyond gloppy, more like a yogurt puddle. And anyway, it seemed wrong to eat it in front of Bess.

"Well," she said as the bell rang. "Thanks for eating with me."

"Sure. Save me a seat tomorrow, okay?"

She shrugged. "Why not," she said.

Somehow, it wasn't exactly what I'd thought she'd say, but I liked hearing it anyway.

seventeen

At dismissal two incredibly weird things happened, one right after the other.

The first happened when I was at the bike rack, unlocking my bike for the ride home. Only about six kids used the rack because everybody else took the bus. But I never did because my bus (Bus 8) went down my old street, and I couldn't stand to pass my old house every day. It made me feel a million ways whenever I saw it, but sad and angry were at the very top of the list. Besides, the new owners had painted our blue house yellow, and it just looked completely wrong.

Anyway, I was unlocking my bike, when I dropped my key right smack in a pile of muddy, slimy oak leaves. "TURD AND A HALF!" I yelled, dropping to the ground to grope through the squishy mess.

And then, who should walk right up to me but Sir Mullvo himself.

"Cassie," he sneered. "Your way with words never fails to impress."

What was the Crayola word for the probable color of my face? Crimson? Magenta? Burnt sienna? "Hi, Mr. Mullaney," I croaked.

"You appear to be looking for something. May I help?"

"Thanks, but you don't have to," I said quickly. "This stuff is disgusting to touch."

"I take it you're not doing it for fun, then. What exactly are you looking for?"

"My bike key," I said, groping frantically now. "I heard it drop. It's got to be here someplace."

"That stands to reason," he agreed, crouching. "You take that pile, and I'll take this one."

And there he was, squooshing his long bony fingers through the sloppy leaves, right beside me. We didn't talk, we just concentrated on squooshing, until finally he got this funny sort of satisfied look on his face.

"Aha! Is this it?" He held up my key like it was Excalibur.

"Yes it is! Thanks a *lot*, Mr. Mullaney!"

He stood up slowly, then winced a little, like something hurt. "You're very welcome. You know, there's a great book you'll read when you're an English major in college. It's about many things, one of which is the keylessness of the hero."

"The *what?*"

"The keylessness, Cassie. He can't find his key."

"Sounds like a fascinating book," I said, thinking, Well, what kind of book did I *expect* Mr. Let's-Get-Cracking to read for fun?

"Anyway," Mr. Mullaney continued, moving his shoulders up and down, like he was testing them out, "his quandary resonates because everyone feels keyless at some point in their lives. There's never anything wrong with asking for help, Cassie. See you tomorrow."

And then he turned toward the faculty parking lot and walked away stiffly, still checking to see if both his shoulders worked.

I just stood there, watching him, wiping my slimy hands on my jeans. If that wasn't the insanest conversation on record, I don't know what was.

And maybe ten seconds later the second weird thing happened.

Just as I was getting on my bike, I heard someone call out, "Hey, Cassie!" I turned around, but the only person I saw standing there was Danny Abbott. I tried looking past him, to see who could have been calling my name, but then he started walking closer. "Hey," he said.

"Hey."

"So, was that just *Mr. Mullaney*?"

"Yeah. He actually helped me look for my bike key. In the *mud*."

"No way."

"And he gave me a speech about resonating quandaries. And books about keys."

Danny shook his head. "The guy's a total freak show," he said, laughing. Then his face changed. Now he looked like *he* was concentrating on finding a bike key in a big pile of muddy leaves. "So, Cassie, is this your bike?"

"Well, either that or I'm stealing it."

A funny look crossed his face then, like he was confused. *Fabulous, Cassie. So he thinks there's a fifty-fifty chance you're a criminal. Way to go.*

"So, I mean, do you ever ride it? Besides to school?"

"Not a lot," I said truthfully. "Sometimes."

"Do you ever ride in Bradley Park?"

Bradley Park is right by my old house. That would be the last place I'd go for a ride, actually.

"No," I said. "Do you?"

"Not really. But some kids do."

"Oh."

Well, thanks for the fascinating travelogue, but now what?

"Okay, well, see you," he muttered. He walked away fast, like he was summoning superhuman power not to run.

What exactly was the point of that entire conversation? Danny could be so weird sometimes. I strapped on my bike helmet, which I hoped would stop my head from exploding, and then I zoomed off for home.

eighteen

<u>The Funniest Words in the English Language</u>

English sure is a funny language. It's full of words that are silly, strange, and just plain weird. Here is a partial list: banana, picnic, squash, squiggle, squeegee, scrunchie, squelch, squirm, squirt, octopus, umbrella, placebo, lollipop, scissors, splurge, obtuse, acute, kumquat, snub, snoop, snore, snort, nostril, fuzz, elbow, knee, thumb, phlegm, stomach, kangaroo, ostrich, aardvark, filibuster, blotch, blemish, cranny, nook, quirk, quark, noodle, egg, giblet, parsnip, marshmallow, parallel, trapezoid, perpendicular,

"Cassie, what are you writing?"

I spun around in my desk chair. Miranda was standing

right behind me, peering over my shoulder, grinning.

"It's your secret diary, isn't it? What's that, a list of all the boys you secretly like?"

"I don't *do* that, Miranda," I said, trying to spread my fingers over the pages so they were completely covered. "And even if I did, I wouldn't tell *you*."

"Why not? You could trust me. I wouldn't tease."

"Ha!"

"Come on, Cassie. Let me see it." She suddenly snatched the journal from under my hands. "'Aardvark, filibuster, blotch, blemish.' What *is* this?"

My face burned. "Nothing! It's private, Miranda!"

"A private list of *words*? Are you psycho?"

"No, Miranda, I'm not! You wouldn't understand."

"Yeah, that my little sister is spending all her time locked in her room writing lists of 'funny words'? You bet I don't understand! Do your friends know about this?" She pointed accusingly at my journal.

I grimaced. "What friends?"

"Halley's Comet and Banana. Those girls you used to hang out with at the pool, remember?"

"Well, I don't go to the pool anymore, and I don't hang out with them either."

"Good. I never liked them. I always thought they were nasty, to be perfectly honest."

"You did? Then why didn't you say anything?"

She snorted. "Because, knowing you, you would have defended them and told me to mind my own business."

"Yeah," I agreed. "That's right. And that's exactly what I'm saying now!" I reached for the journal, but she snapped her arm behind her, hiding it from me.

"So, don't you hang out with *anyone*?"

"That's personal information, Miranda!"

"Whoa, calm down. Why are you so touchy?"

"Because I'm trying to concentrate!"

"On your 'list'? I'm really starting to worry about you, Cassie."

"Listen, Miranda," I said in my Authority Figure voice, "it's a project for school, and you'd better give it back right now, or you'll be sorry!"

Suddenly the doorbell was ringing. And ringing and ringing.

Miranda glared at me, like it was my fault. "*I'll* get it," she muttered. She tossed the journal back on my desk and stomped out of my room.

Thirty seconds later she was back, making meaningful

eye contact, which I totally didn't get. Then immediately I did, when I saw she was being followed by Mrs. Patella and her invisible cloud of stinky cigarettes.

"Everything all right, Cassie?" Mrs. Patella asked, her eyes darting all around my messy room.

"Yes, of course, Mrs. Patella," I said. "Why?"

"Why? Well, I could hear you girls yelling at each other through the walls. They're so thin, you can hear everything, and you know I promised your mother I'd keep an eye on you. So, I was just checking in to make sure everything was all right. *Is* everything all right?" Eyes still darting.

"Yes, Mrs. Patella, sure."

"Well, you know I worry about you kids here all alone while your mother—"

"We're not 'all alone,' we're here *together*," Miranda interrupted. "And we were just having a little tiff, like normal siblings. So, thanks for dropping by, but *we're fine.*"

"Yup," I said, all cheery. "Thanks anyway, Mrs. Patella!"

She was barely out the door, trailing cigarette smoke behind her, when Miranda and I both started giggling. First giggling, then laughing. Then hooting and whooping so hard our faces were red and our eyes were tearing and our stomachs hurt. Laughing so hard we ended up rolling on my bed, holding our sides.

"A 'tiff'? A *tiff*? Where did you get that from?" I shrieked.

"I don't know," Miranda gasped. "England?"

We started laughing again. I was hot and sweaty and my sides ached. I could barely breathe.

"'A little tiff, like normal siblings'? Why did you call us 'siblings'? Why not sisters?"

"I don't know," she said, trying to catch her breath. "It just sounded more impressive."

"What a funny word," I said. "Siblings. *Siblings.* It sounds like giblets." I started laughing again, but weakly.

"Cassie, you have issues," said Miranda, getting up. She stretched her arms like she was yawning onstage, then shook out her long hair.

I watched her. My hair was incapable of being shook out; it was just barely long enough for a scrunchie. Miranda's hair was nice. Too bad that wasn't genetic. "Miranda?" I said, all of a sudden. "Can I ask you a question?"

"Maybe. What?"

"What do you think happened to Dad?"

She sat back down on my bed. “What? Whatever made you think of *that*?”

“I don’t know,” I said slowly. “Maybe when you told Mrs. Patella that we’re all together. We aren’t, are we.”

“Yes we are! *He’s* just not in the family anymore.”

“But why? What do you think happened?

She looked at me, then sighed. “Do we really have to talk about this right now?”

“Well, yeah. I mean, why not now? We never talk about him, Miranda.”

“That’s because there’s nothing to say. He just disappeared.”

“But *why*?”

She didn’t answer. Finally, she sort-of-coughed a couple of times. “I’m not sure. I mean, I don’t know this for a fact or anything, but I think it may have had something to do with money.”

“Really? Why do you think that?”

“I don’t know. I’ve just been thinking about fights I heard between Mom and Dad, all this arguing about where the money went. And once I overheard Mom talking to Aunt Abby about money being gone from the bank.”

"Well, that could be anything—"

"Maybe," Miranda interrupted. "I really don't know. Every time I ask Mom, she says something like, 'I know this is awful for you, honey, but Dad really has to explain this himself.' And since the phone isn't exactly ringing off the hook with his quote-unquote *explanations*, maybe we'll never know."

"Well," I said carefully, "you know, he did call, Miranda. He called three times in August, but you hung up on him."

"That's because he never had anything to say! He just wanted *us* to do all the talking."

"Yeah, well, he might have said more if you hadn't hung up."

"If he had anything else to say, Cassie, he would've called back!"

"Maybe. Unless he thought we were too mad. And that maybe we didn't *want* to hear from him."

Her eyes flashed. "Oh, so what are you saying? That I don't have the right to be angry? That it's all *my* fault he doesn't call?"

"Come on, Ran," I said. "That's not what I meant." But it sort of was, and I didn't want to start a war right then, so I quickly changed the subject. "Let me talk to Mom next time. I never ask because I don't want to get her all upset, but maybe she'll tell me something."

"Oh yeah, right, Casshead. Like she'd tell you but not me."

"She might."

"Oh, I'm sure."

Neither of us said anything for a really long time. I picked four fuzzballs off my old red sweater. Finally I asked a big question.

"Do you think maybe Dad has a new family?" It was something I often wondered about, but this was the first time I'd ever asked it out loud.

Miranda snorted. "Why? He had a perfectly good old one, and he didn't want it anymore. To tell you the truth, I don't really care *what* he does."

"It doesn't bother you?"

"Sometimes. But I've got too much else bothering me. Like my *sibling*." She poked me in the rib. It sort of tickled.

"Sibling. Sibling. Sib-ling. It *is* a weird word, isn't it?"

"Bizarre," said Miranda, getting up again. "So take it. My gift. Add it to your psycho word list, Casshead."

nineteen

That night I couldn't fall asleep, even though I had both cats on my bed, purring in stereo. Miranda's theory about why Dad left was tumbling around and around in my head like dirty clothes in a washing machine. I couldn't stop thinking about it, even though I kept ordering myself to just switch it off, space out, picture puffy clouds in a big blue sky.

Something to do with money.

Like what, exactly? How could anything to do with money make a person suddenly get up and leave his family and go off to somewhere, possibly to Florida, maybe forever? And then stop wanting "to hear our voices" just because Miranda got mad and hung up a few times? It made absolutely no sense.

Because Dad didn't even seem to care about money. He

never gave pointlessly boring lectures about Thrift and Saving and Investing, the way Brianna's father did. And we always seemed to have enough, maybe not a ton of money like some people in Emerson, but enough for us. More than enough, really, when you counted Disneyland and Utah and the fitness club. I mean, money just never seemed to be an issue.

Unless maybe it was.

Maybe even all along. And maybe I just never realized it.

I guess you don't notice everything when it's happening.

Even if you're smart.

I punched my pillow.

Okay, I yelled at myself, *so THINK, Cassie.* Wasn't there some incident, some clue, some kind of flashing neon warning sign that Dad was having money trouble? Or any other kind of trouble, for that matter?

There had to be, but I couldn't think of any. From what I remembered he seemed pretty normal before he left: sitting in front of the TV on Sundays watching what he called "college hoops." Playing incredibly loud guitar music from, like, the 1970s. Working late all the time. Reading.

Reading.

Suddenly I thought of something, but it probably wasn't important. At least, I didn't think it was. But I couldn't stop it sloshing around in my mind. It's like my mental washing machine was on automatic, and all I could do was watch the suds.

One morning last spring, maybe a week before he was officially "out of the picture," Dad was racing out the kitchen door to catch his train. He hadn't even bothered to eat breakfast; he just mumbled that he'd "grab something" on the way to work. And then, just as he was leaving, he stopped to open his bulging briefcase on the kitchen table. Then he started flipping through a thick bunch of papers.

"Hey, Dad," I remember saying through a mouth full of soggy Cheerios. "Can I have ten dollars for the fitness club? There's a new swim shop—"

"Not now," he snapped, without looking at me. "I'm busy, Cassie. Can't you tell?"

"Sorry."

I ate my Cheerios while he read his papers. Then I said, a bit louder this time, "The thing is, Dad, I desperately need new goggles. My old ones ripped, so can I please just buy a new pair?"

He stared at me in disbelief, as if I'd just asked him for two new eyeballs.

"Not now," he repeated. "Do you think I'm a bank?"

He stuffed the papers back into his briefcase, but there were so many of them that this time it wouldn't close. I heard him mutter a word I wasn't supposed to hear, then he reached into his briefcase and took out a small, thick paperback, one of the "airport books" that he liked to read on the train. Then he did the ugliest thing I'd ever seen in my entire life.

He ripped it in half.

Right along the spine.

Then he tossed half the book in the trash. And he stuffed the other half into his briefcase, which now clicked shut.

"DAD!" I shrieked at him. "What did you just do?"

He sort of shrugged. "Oh, that. Just an old packing trick, Cassie. Cuts down on bulk."

"But, Dad! It's a book! How could you rip a book?"

"Oh, come on, Cassie, don't make such a big deal. I do it all the time. Anyway, it's an airport book, remember?"

"Yes, but you *like* airport books!"

Now he put his hand on my shoulder. "Of course I do,

Cassie, I like them a lot, but they're not important, they're just to pass the time."

My throat was getting croaky. "But what if you want to reread it someday?"

"I never do."

"But what if someone else does?"

"Listen," he said, taking his hand back. "I really need to catch my train. There's a lot going on at work, and I can't afford to be late. Okay, Cassie? You need some money?"

I shook my head.

"Here's twenty dollars," he said, slapping a bill on the table. "Buy what you want."

"Never mind, Dad. I'm fine."

"Just take it, Cassie."

Then he ran out. I remember staring at the maimed little half-book sitting in the trash, but I didn't fish it out because, really, what was the point? But now it seemed huge to me. Because I couldn't stop wondering: Is that what he did to us—just threw us away, like an old packing trick?

And what about how weird he'd acted, all jumpy and distracted? And asking if I thought he was a bank—he *never* said things like that. Did it have something to do with the missing money? Or with the fights Miranda overheard about "where the money went"? Or all those "private discussions" I kept barging in on all the time?

I re-punched my pillow. *Okay, now stop it,* I told myself. *Get a grip. This is DAD we're talking about, remember?*

That was when I absolutely forced myself to remember all the nice things about him. Stuff I hadn't allowed inside my brain for the last seven months.

Like how he took us bowling, and pretended to throw gutter balls so Jackson wouldn't feel bad. How he always gave us an extra scoop of ice cream if we said "please." How he helped me practice my multiplication tables, and never got impatient with me, even though I couldn't remember eight times six, no matter how hard I tried. How he was practically the only parent on our street who wore a costume on Halloween. How he always wrote each kid a silly poem for our birthday. I still remember the one he wrote for me when I turned eleven:

Happy birthday, dearest Cassie
Never was a nicer lassie.
Feisty, funny, spunky, sassy,
Here's to you, O daughter Cassie.

By now my eyes were stinging and my throat was feeling tight. I didn't want to cry. If I cried, I thought, everything would just come crashing down, like the little pins on the Queen's Battle Map. And then who would there be to pick them up? Miranda? Oh, right, *sure.*

And besides, how can you defend somebody when you're crying?

I looked at my watch: eleven forty-five. I needed something to do, since obviously sleeping wasn't an option. So I poked Buster. "Get up, you fat cat, and I'll feed you," I whispered.

He opened one eye and glared at me. No one gives a dirty look better than a cat.

"Listen, Buster, if I were you, I'd take that offer," I said more loudly. "You never know where your next meal is coming from."

Cats are smart. And practical. He followed me into the kitchen, followed by Fuzzy, who always demanded equal service.

I opened the cabinet where we kept the cans of cat food. Only three left: good thing Mom was doing the shopping tomorrow, because I certainly didn't want to have to deal with nagging Miranda. I was just about to open a can of Turkey & Giblets when I heard a funny buzzing sound coming from the living room.

"Hold on, you guys," I murmured, taking the can with me in case I had to hurl something at a burglar's head.

But there was no burglar. Just Miranda, sprawling on the sofa with a bowl of Extra Spicy Doritos on her chest, watching music videos on our buzzy old TV.

"Hi, Cash," she said, her mouth all orange. "Wanna watch?"

"How can I?" I said, sitting down on the little patch of sofa that wasn't taken over by Miranda's smelly feet. "The TV's broken. You can't even hear anything."

"Duh. I asked if you wanted to *watch.*"

"Okay. Just a little, maybe."

She drew up her knees to make room for me. "Why are you even up?"

"I couldn't sleep. I was thinking about all that stuff you said about Dad. Why are *you* up?"

"I'm always up," she replied. "Mom's so wiped out she wouldn't know if I watched MTV all night." She grinned evilly. "Or did something else."

"Well, don't get any ideas," I grumbled. "Hand over the chips."

"Take the whole bowl. I'm stuffed." She sat up. "Listen, Cass, I didn't mean to upset you by talking about Dad. I don't even *know* anything."

"Anyway, you're wrong," I said, staring at the screen. "There's no way he would do it."

"Do what?"

"You know. *Steal*."

Miranda looked at me like I was speaking Javanese. "What are you talking about, Cassie? I never said anything about stealing!"

"You said money was gone from the bank."

"Right. And I said *I didn't know what happened*. But if you really want, I'll tell you what I *think*."

I nodded.

"What I *think* is that Dad lost a lot of money somehow, and he's ashamed, and that's why he isn't in touch with us. I have absolutely no proof, but one day I'm going to ask Aunt Abby, and if she says I'm right, then I'll just tell Mom I know. And I'll tell you, too, if you want."

"Well, *sure*. Of course!"

"Fine. But even if I'm right about this, it still makes him wrong, and I still hate him."

"You shouldn't hate him, Miranda. He's *Dad*. Remember

those Halloween costumes? And those birthday poems?"

"He had no right to just disappear," she snapped, "and no right to pretend we don't exist *now*." She stood up then, and started brushing Doritos crumbs off her pj's.

"But he loves us, so if he needed to do that, don't you think he must have had a really, really good reason?" I demanded.

"Yeah, well, have fun in fantasyland," Miranda said. "I'm turning in. Are you still watching the TV?"

"Yeah," I said. "I guess I will. For a while."

"Well, feed the cats, then," she said. "Good night."

twenty

Friday was payday, and Mom did a mega-shopping expedition after work. Miranda had nuked us some Stouffer's and then run out the door—guess where—to Madison's ("Tell Mom I'll be back by ten!"). That meant Jackson and I had to help Mom haul in the shopping bags when she drove up at nine fifteen. When we used to live in our big house with Dad, I used to hate putting away groceries. But now that everything was different and groceries were, like, this major issue, I couldn't believe how great it felt to be putting away normal things like eggs and hamburger and bananas. Even Jackson, who was already in his pj's and ready for bed, hopped around the kitchen like an excited bunny.

"Oreos, hurray! Oreos, hurray!" he sang.

Mom gave him a big smoochy kiss, then put him to

bed. A few minutes later she came into the living room. "Cassie, can I talk to you a minute?"

That made me a little nervous. "Sure."

"Sit, honey. I wanted to talk with you about how things are going around here lately."

"What things?"

"You know, the whole routine. Chores, homework, cooking, everything. I've been working so late that I feel like I'm out of touch with you."

I swallowed. Here was my chance to tell her everything, especially about Miranda, but for some reason I still couldn't do it. This was a big mystery to me, even as I sat there on the couch with Mom. She had practically handed me an invitation to squeal on my lazy, selfish, irresponsible sister, and here I was just sitting there, pulling fuzzballs off my old red sweater.

"Cassie, stop doing that to your sweater," Mom scolded.

I looked up at her. She had dark shadows under her eyes, and not from no-clump mascara. And I could see a few silvery threads in her brown hair. I'd never noticed them before. Were they recent? They definitely made her look older, but I sort of liked them. "Everything's fine," I said. "Really. But I was just thinking that it might be better if you always took care of all the shopping."

"Why?" she challenged. "Has Miranda not been keeping up?"

"No, *no,* it's just that sometimes it's hard for her to shop after school, with her busy schedule and everything. I guess we're just eating a lot these days."

She weighed what I said. "Okay, then. Fine. I do think this is something Miranda should be able to handle, but fine. From now on I'll just leave Miranda to look after Jackson and cook supper. Thanks for telling me, Cassie."

She paused. When she spoke again, her voice had that strangled sound, like mine did when I asked Mr. Mullaney if he'd even read my story. "Listen, honey, I'm really sorry things have been so tight these past few weeks. I know we've been running low on things, and I know that the TV needs fixing. It's just that we've had a lot of big bills this month, but they're all paid now, and things will be better. Okay?"

She was *asking* me? "Okay."

And then my heart started bumping around in my chest because I was thinking, *All right, Cassie, this is when you demand information about Dad.* But the words just clotted up in my throat, and I sat there like a barf-brained blob.

"Good, then. So how's school?"

Should I tell her? What for? It was all so insanely stupid and mindless anyway. "Fine."

"And how are Hayley and Brianna? I haven't seen them in a while."

Imagine that. Why do you think that is, Mom? "They're fine. Just really busy with swim team. Oh, by the way, have you spoken to Jackson's teacher yet? She keeps calling here."

Mom blew out some air. "Yes, she called me at the office twice. I tried calling her back this afternoon, but she'd already left school for the day. I'll try again first thing Monday morning. Why, has Jackie said what this is about?"

Another chance for me to talk. But after blowing it with Miranda, I had to be careful, so that Mom wouldn't also think I needed to "get a life." "Not really," I said. "But I think he may be struggling a bit with his reading. I'm not sure."

She blinked. "Well, yes he is, but it's being addressed. Mrs. Rivera is an excellent teacher, and she's working very hard with him."

"Really?"

"Oh, yes. You know, reading is hard for some kids at first. Not everyone is as precocious as you were!" She smiled at me, then stood up. "What time did Miranda say she was getting back from Madison's? We have a busy day tomorrow."

"I'm not sure." She'd said ten, of course, but it was already nine fifty-five, so I thought I'd just give her a few extra minutes to walk in the door. Knowing Miranda, she probably needed every second she could get.

"Well, I'm turning in. I'm absolutely *exhausted.*" She kissed me, not the same kind of smoochy kiss she'd given Jackson. Then she looked me right in the eyes. "Thanks again, Cassie. I know I can really count on you," she said.

And she went to bed, and didn't hear Miranda walk in the door at two fifteen a.m.

twenty-one

Weekends were all pretty much the same for us. On Saturdays, Mom "slept in," which meant she got up around seven thirty, then read the newspaper and drank big mugs of coffee. Then we ran around shopping for socks or screwdrivers or random boring things like that. Sometimes we had haircuts, sometimes we went to the orthodontist, which was like this big middle-school hangout, especially on Saturdays. (Once I saw Danny Abbott there, but he pretended not to notice me.) And at four we took Jackson to the rec field in town for his soccer game, the one extracurricular activity we kept in our schedule, because it was free.

Then Mom cooked us a real dinner, not some radioactive microwaved box of a dinner like we ate during the week. Then we did mountains of laundry, and sort-of-watched a video. Sometimes Mom and Jackson fell asleep on the couch before it was even over.

Every other Sunday morning we all piled into our old Caravan and headed ninety minutes north to visit Grandpop in his nursing home. I kind of dreaded this, to be honest, because he barely recognized us anymore. But it was really important to Mom, so we never complained, not even Jackson, who was just a toddler when Grandpop had his stroke. About once a month we drove up to Aunt Abby's house, which was another hour from the nursing home. Aunt Abby's house was always great: Jackie and I usually got to play outside with our cousins, Cody, who was eleven, and Nell, who was nine. We did stuff like fish for minnows in a stream they had in the back of their house, and in the winter we went sledding and snowboarding down this incredibly steep hill and had huge snowball fights.

Miranda kept insisting I was too old to be playing like this. But what was I supposed to do, yak on the phone and practice putting on no-clump mascara? Lock myself in a room, crank up some stupid "music," and dream about Danny Abbott? I *loved* playing with my cousins, and being in a real house again, with a real backyard. I didn't care what Miranda or the stupid Hayley-Brianna-Lindsay voice in my head kept saying. Aunt Abby's house was where I felt like I could *breathe.*

Early, like around five, Aunt Abby and Uncle Keith would make us a big supper, and Mom would actually look relaxed and happy while we all crammed ourselves around the table. Cody would tell these really dumb, complicated jokes that everyone would groan at, but then everyone would try to top him with even dumber jokes that all ended up sounding the same. We always had ice cream for dessert, even when it was cold out, and Mom always had a coffee "for the road." Then we'd clear the table, hug and kiss good-bye, get in the car, and drive all the way back to our ratty little "unit," which was definitely the saddest, longest, worst car ride you can imagine.

But this weekend was different. For starters, Miranda didn't get up until noon on Saturday. This wasn't exactly surprising, considering how late she'd come home on Friday. I didn't think Mom knew what time Miranda had finally shown up, but then I heard Mom go into Miranda's room to wake her. They had a huge fight about being responsible and obeying curfew and deserving trust, blah blah blah.

When Miranda finally came out of her room, she looked furious. "You are so dead," she hissed at me.

"Why? What did I do?"

"You don't know? I'll tell you later."

Jackson and I did the Saturday thing with Mom (bank, Blockbuster, library, soccer) while Miranda stayed in her room playing "music" behind her shut door. Right before supper she stomped into my room.

"So, I'm not doing the shopping? I'm not being 'responsible'?"

"I never said that! Did Mom say I said that?"

"I never go shopping on the way home from school? Who just the other day went out and filled the freezer? Who bought peanut butter and cat food and Ring Dings, which just miraculously 'disappeared' when Madison came over?"

"Miranda, I never said you were irresponsible. I could have, you know I could. But I didn't. I *chose* not to."

"Oh, really?"

"Yes, really! I was actually covering up for you, for some stupid reason!"

"Oh yeah, well, thanks a lot. Now I'm grounded for a month, thanks to how you 'covered up' for me!"

"Listen, Miranda," I said. "It's not my fault you came home last night at two fifteen, without telling anyone where you were! You knew that was wrong! Mom has every right to punish you for that!"

Miranda looked shocked for a second. Then she exploded. Totally exploded.

"Oh yeah, Cassie, there you go again, judging everybody else's 'problems.' You're just on your own perfect little planet, aren't you? Well, let me tell you something: You really do need to get a life, and one of these days you'll realize it, instead of sitting in your little room doing your 'homework,' or your psycho 'word lists' or whatever it is you're writing all the time, instead of having any *friends.* That's what it is, isn't it—you're really just jealous of me because I have friends, and you don't, *right*?"

"What? What are you talking about?"

"You know exactly what I'm talking about! You just hide behind your desk and criticize everything I do! And it's so easy for you, isn't it, Cassie, because you're just sitting there by yourself *scribbling,* while I have to deal with all this academic pressure and try to have some kind of social life, even though I can't *do* anything or *go* anywhere because I have to come home every afternoon and shop and babysit and cook supper and then on weekends visit boring relatives I don't even have anything in common with!"

"But, Miranda, listen. You offered to watch Jackie, it was *your idea*, remember?"

"Yeah, well, you always have an answer, don't you, Cassie."

Then she stomped out of my room.

On Sunday she didn't come with us to visit Grandpop and Aunt Abby.

And that week, for some weird reason, it wasn't even fun.

twenty-two

On Monday morning Mom took a big gulp of coffee, then frowned. "Okay, Miranda. You'll be coming home straight from school today, and not going to Madison's under any circumstances. For supper you're making hamburgers and baked potatoes, and there are greens I already washed for a salad."

Miranda glared at her, then chomped on her burnt bagel.

"And Jackie, I need to call Mrs. Rivera back this morning. Did anything happen at school on Friday that I need to know about?"

"Not really," Jackson said. He poked his Cheerios with his spoon.

"What does *that* mean?"

He shrugged. "I don't know."

Mom looked at me for help, but I just looked back at her like, *Dang if I know!*

"Okay, then," she said in her back-to-business voice. "I'm going to miss my train."

Then she got up, blew us a group kiss, and left. Miranda immediately dumped her bagel into the garbage and stormed into the bathroom.

"Is Miranda mad?" Jackie asked.

"Who knows," I snarled. "Time to get ready for school, Jackie boy."

I helped him pack his Spider-Man backpack, then stood with him in the Shady Woods driveway to wait for his bus. (Usually this was Miranda's job, but she was still locked in the bathroom, probably gnashing her teeth and putting on no-clump mascara.) Of course, the bus chose this morning to be four minutes late, so once Jackson finally got on and gave me a combination pout/good-bye wave through the window, I had exactly six minutes to zoom on my bike to school.

First period was Math, which today meant converting fractions to percents. We did that back in fifth grade, and then again in sixth, and here we were in seventh grade, and we were *still* converting fractions to percents. You'd think they'd all be converted by now, but apparently not. While Mrs. Gillroy was writing on the whiteboard, I slipped my journal out of my backpack.

Forty-seven pages since the last journal check. Despite what Bess Waterbury had said to me at lunch that time, I was still going to keep filling pages with totally boneheaded nothingness, at this point purely out of spite. I uncapped my black extra-fine-point Rolling Writer.

<u>The Complete List of Occasions When Converting Fractions into Percents Comes in Handy</u>

Hmmm . . . well, for starters, there's . . . no, that's not one. Well, then, there's always . . . no, not that, either. Well, there's always . . . no, come to think of it, you really <u>don't</u> need to convert fractions to percents to write fantasy novels. Maybe you did in the prehistoric pre-calculator days, but not anymore.

Oh dear. Maybe you NEVER need to convert fractions to percents to live a normal, productive life on planet Earth. Maybe this is just a pathetically unnecessary waste of time, after all. Maybe this is just an incredibly mindless exercise for pathetically boring kids (who/whom) one day, if they study hard enough, will become pathetically boring Math teachers.

Mrs. Gillroy started handing back a pop quiz. I knew I'd bombed it; no suspense there. Then she handed me mine: a 72. "Cassie, you can do much better! See me if you want some help!" she wrote next to the grade. "Thanks, but I'm busy writing novels," I wrote back.

Then I flipped to the next page in my journal:

YOOHOO! (HOOM!) ANYBODY HOME?

Whom really cares about who? Whom works on a stupid English assignment (which, that) everyone whom knows anything thinks is a total waste of time, ink, and paper? Whom really cares? Whom is reading this? No one, that's whom.

I can write anything (that, which) I want, and nobody will even notice. Especially not you, Mr. Mullaney, because you don't notice ANYTHING.

You just count pages, don't you? Like this: one two three four five six! Seven eight nine ten eleven! What comes next? Twelve? Thirteen! No, fourteen! Wow! Counting pages is oodles of fun! Tralalalalala. I'm just filling S P A C E . . . with words. Words words words words words words words. More words. More words. Even more words.

Wore mords.

Wordy words. Wordy words–words. Wordy wordy wordy words. Words? Words! WORDS! WORDS!! WORDS!!! WORDS!!!!

(Words. Wordswordswordswordswords.)

Words are weird. Why, for example, do people say tuna fish? They don't say salmon fish or halibut fish or mackerel fish or sardine fish, but they do say tuna fish. Is "fish" totally necessary? You don't say hamburger beef or chicken poultry. So why do you say tuna FISH like you have to specify what it is? This makes absolutely no sense. Except, of course, if you order it in the lunchroom. Then I guess you really DO need to specify.

What else? What else? Hmmm . . .

Here's what else:

You can tune a piano but you can't tune a fish.

Ha ha ha ha ha ha ha hah hah ha ha. Yessiree, it sure feels good to get that out of my system. There's nothing like a good laugh to make you feel all better. Don't you agree, Mr. Mullaney? Don't you just love to laugh your head off about how POINTLESS and MEANINGLESS everything is, especially this stupid, insulting journal assignment? Yup, laughter truly is the best medicine. At least that's what they say. I think I'll laugh some more: HA HA HA HA HA HA HA! Heee, heee, heee! HAH! HAH! HAH! HAH! He, he, he, he, he, he! Heh, heh, heh, heh, heh! hahahahahahahahahahahaha!!!!!!!!!!!!!! HO HO HO, MERRY CHRISTMAS!

When the bell rang, it was time for English. And when Mr. Mullaney sneeringly announced a journal check at the end of class, I didn't pass it in. Instead, I brought my journal to the front of the class, and then dropped it on his desk. Just like I'd dropped Fuzzy on Miranda's head.

Whoops. Sentence fragment. Right, Zachary Hogan? Right, Mr. Mullaney? *Right*?

twenty-three

The whole rest of the morning I was turning cartwheels in my head. It felt great to drop the journal on Mr. Mullaney's desk, and even better to imagine his long bony fingers flipping through entry after entry of wordy-word-words, as he mindlessly tallied up the number of pages. *Sixty-three,* he'd sneer. *Cassie, your way with page counts never fails to impress.*

I could just imagine the scene when he handed them back.

"This page number requirement is such a *joke,*" Zachary Hairball would announce. "I got a twenty-seven!"

"That's very good," I'd reply encouragingly. "Of course, *I* got a sixty-three!"

Total mayhem.

I replayed the scene in my head all through Science,

and all through Gym, refilming it from different angles, sometimes with Danny (*"Wow, Cassie, you're amazing!"*), sometimes with Hayley and Brianna (*"We somehow never realized how clever you were, Cassie. Or how amusing. Want to sit with us at lunch today?"*).

But by lunchtime my stomach was starting to feel weird. I can't explain why; it was just jumpy, somehow. So even though I filled up my tray with two cheese enchiladas and another yogurt sundae, when I sat down with Bess, I hardly took a bite.

"Are you okay?" she asked, nibbling her fruit salad.

"Fine," I answered. "I'm just not very hungry, I guess."

I poked an enchilada with a spork. *Spork*, I thought. *Spork. Spork is definitely a funny word. Maybe I'll add it to the funny-word list. When Mr. Mullaney gives me back my journal.*

"Don't sit here if you don't want to, Cassie," Bess said, maybe a little too loudly.

"What?" I looked up at her. "Who said I didn't want to?"

"I don't know. I mean, if you'd rather sit with Hayley and Brianna, go ahead."

"I'd rather pull out my toenails," I answered. And I realized I meant it too.

She giggled. "You aren't friends anymore?"

"I don't think we ever were."

"You hung out with them."

It was almost an accusation. "Well, yes," I said, surprised to be defending myself. "But we had zero in common. Besides swim team, which I dropped."

She speared a suspiciously orange slice of cantaloupe. But she didn't eat it; she seemed to be deciding something. Finally she spoke. "I have those books for you, Cassie. If you still want them."

Oh yeah, right. And no pink cellophane. "You mean the books your mom wants you to get rid of?"

She nodded. "There were too many to bring to school. And I didn't know which ones you wanted. So, maybe you could come over sometime and just take some?" Now she started to blush, which made me feel even weirder. Because how could anybody actually be nervous about inviting groupless loser *me*?

Before I knew what I was doing, I'd agreed to come to her house that very afternoon. There was a pay phone in the outer lobby, and I always kept some quarters in my backpack ("For an emergency," Mom said). So, what I did, also before I knew what I was doing, was call Mrs. Patella.

She answered the phone like she'd been expecting a call from the CIA. "HELLO?"

"Hi, Mrs. Patella? This is Cassie Baldwin."

"CASSIE?"

"Your neighbor. Anne's daughter? I'm sorry to have to ask you this, but I'll be detained at school on a special project. I'm sure Miranda will be home from school at two thirty-five. But on the outside chance she's running late, do you think you could possibly meet Jackson at the bus?"

"A SPECIAL PROJECT?" she repeated.

"Yes," I said, absolutely refusing to give her any more information.

Silence, while she considered. Or smoked a pack of cigarettes.

"Well, what time do you think you'll be home?"

"Three fifteen at the latest," I promised.

"Okay," she agreed, finally. "But he has to come to my house. I'm in the middle of a lot of things right now!"

I bet you are, I thought. *Like bugging my bedroom, for starters.*

I ran back to Bess, who was getting her stuff from her locker. We agreed that she'd take the bus and I'd ride my bike to her house, which was only seven blocks from the school.

We'd lived in Emerson all my life, so it was strange to me to be riding down a street I'd never been on before. But I'd certainly heard of it: Evergreen Road, one of the nicest streets in Emerson, with the biggest, newest, fanciest houses. That horrible Lindsay Frost lived here somewhere, and so did Danny's friend Noah. And I realized it was surprising to me that Bess lived here too, but I couldn't figure out exactly why.

I arrived at her driveway about five minutes before she did, so I had time to study the outside of her cream-colored house and imagine all the rooms. It looked enormous, like one of those houses you see in magazines in the orthodontist's office. Roundish windows, a funny little turret, two separate balconies, possibly a sunroom. The kind of house with a million bathrooms *and* a sauna *and* a home theater with a humungo TV screen that doesn't sound the slightest bit like buzzing bugs. In other words, not a ratty little "unit" like ours.

But not like our old house either. Our old house was pretty big, I always thought, but it was about one tenth the size of this one. And much plainer, too.

And then I started thinking about how nice and cozy it was, and how much I missed it.

Could it just have gotten "lost" somehow, like a bicycle key?

How could you lose a *house*?

There had to be a reason. Maybe I didn't know it yet, but that didn't mean there wasn't one. A really good one.

The bus arrived, and the door opened, and Bess got off looking flushed and happy.

"So you found it!" she exclaimed, out of breath.

"Sure. It was easy."

She opened the front door, and immediately a huge yellow Lab came springing out at us, barking like crazy, leaping up at Bess, and then at me, and then at Bess again.

"Rudy, NO!" she commanded, grabbing the dog's front paws and forcing him down. Then he looked up at her sweetly, and wagged his tail.

"I'm sorry, Cassie," Bess said, laughing. "Rudy's actually only ten months old, but he's an obedience school dropout. We're getting a private tutor to teach him some manners, *aren't we*?"

Rudy jumped up again, and licked her face.

I laughed too, but I was thinking: Rudy is another surprise.

Then she led me up to her bedroom, which was somehow *not* a surprise. It was like a personal, private library, with shelf after shelf of paperbacks, and one whole bookcase filled with fancy hardcovers, the kind you get for your birthday. She had a big white desk *not* covered with gum wrappers and Post-its, and her own personal laptop. Her bed had a special clamp-on reading lamp and one of those enormous pillows so you can read in bed without leaning on your elbow. And the walls were painted a light sky blue, so you felt like you were drifting on a cloud of books.

Fantasyland.

"I love this room," I breathed. "Bess, you are so, so lucky!"

"Thanks," she said simply. "Well, why don't you see what you want? Mom's working in her office upstairs, and I just need to tell her I'm home. I'll be back in a second, okay?"

Of course it was okay. I walked up and down the shelves, taking down books, putting them back. Bess was exaggerating only a teeny bit when she told me she had millions of fantasy novels. She had all the good ones, plus tons I'd never even heard of. I wanted everything, but finally I took only three paperbacks, because I had to cram them into my bulging backpack and I wasn't exactly about to use Dad's "old packing trick." I was struggling with the zipper when Bess walked back into the room.

"I'm taking a Robin McKinley and two Diana Wynne Joneses," I told her.

"Sure. You can take more if you want, Cassie."

"Thanks, but my backpack's totally stuffed! It's a good thing we handed in those journals today, otherwise I'd have no room for even these!"

She groaned. "Don't mention the *J* word."

"Why not?"

"Because I had almost nothing to turn in this time."

I looked up at her. "I thought you told me you were writing a novel."

"Well, yes, I am, but I decided it was too personal to show Mr. Mullaney. Even though he can be sort of nice."

"WHAT?"

She started giggling. "Okay, I know, I know, he's really weird. But the other day I showed him these poems I wrote, and he said he really liked them, and that maybe I should submit one to the school literary magazine."

I didn't know why, but it was very hard to speak right then. "Great!" I said. "So, will you?"

"Maybe. I can't decide which, though. Maybe I can show them to you and you can help me pick?"

"Sure! Well, I think I'd better go now. My neighbor's watching my little brother for me."

"Okay, well, thanks for coming," she said, looking a little unsure. Maybe she thought I was racing out of her house. Maybe I was.

And the whole time I rode home in the freezing November afternoon, I was thinking to myself: *Sixty-three pages, Cassie. Sixty-three whopping pages.*

twenty-four

The first thing I did when I got home from Bess's house was check Miranda's room. She wasn't there, of course. It was exactly ten after three, and since this morning Mom had *ordered* her to come straight home from school, that meant she was thirty-five minutes late. Not a good sign.

And really bad for me. Because I couldn't be here right now. I had something important to do for once, and I absolutely couldn't be sitting around the "unit" babysitting my little brother.

Sometimes you just have to leave.

My heart was pounding as I banged on Mrs. Patella's door.

"CASSIE?" she guessed, as she peeped through the peephole.

"YES!" I shouted back. That must have alarmed her,

because she opened the door without first asking a zillion follow-up questions.

I took a step into her "unit." It felt like I was walking into an ashtray.

"How's Jackson?" I panted.

"Fine," she replied, staring at me. "We're playing chess."

"Chess?"

"He's very good. He says they taught him to play at school."

"Jackson's playing *chess*?"

I ran into her living room, which was exactly the same as ours, same windows, same slanted ceiling—except hers was smoggy from cigarette smoke. I practically needed a searchlight to find Jackson, but there he was, sitting at her coffee table, his head resting on his fists, studying a chessboard.

"Hey, Jackie boy!" I greeted him, probably a bit too enthusiastically.

He didn't look up. Maybe he was angry at me for leaving him here. Maybe he just expected it. After all, everyone else had abandoned him. Why should I be any different?

I felt like a total skuzzball. Still, *I had something important to do.*

"Listen, Jackie, do you think you could stay here for, like, fifteen more minutes?" I whispered to him. "Maybe twenty at the most?"

"I don't care," he said, still refusing to look at me. "Do what you want. Mrs. Patella is making brownies."

I didn't even want to *think* about eating brownies in this stinky house. "Okay, then, be good," I said. "Try to hear if Miranda gets home."

Now he looked up. "How will I know?"

"Just listen through the walls," I said. "Or ask Mrs. Patella."

Then I raced to the kitchen, where sure enough Mrs. Patella was taking a tray of slightly burnt brownies out of the oven. "Would you like one, Cassie?" she asked skeptically.

"No!" I practically shouted. "I mean, *thanks,* but I'm in a big rush. I just realized I have to get back to school for a second."

She narrowed her eyes at me. "For your special project?"

"Yes! That's right, I need something for my project, and I have to go back and get it."

"Weelll," she said slowly. "How long will this take?"

"Ten minutes. Maybe fifteen. And Miranda should be back any second."

"Where is she? I thought you said she'd be back by now."

"She must have gotten held up." My heart was practically leaping out of my chest. It seemed crazy to me that she couldn't see it.

"Weelll, okay," Mrs. Patella finally decided. "But come straight back. I've got other things to do, you know."

"Thanks!" I called, racing out the door, back into the freezing November air, which felt amazingly good after two minutes in that stinky, smoggy, smoky little "unit." I restrapped my bike helmet, got back on my bike, and zoomed back to school.

This is why: I needed to get my journal back. I don't even know what made me decide this. Maybe hearing about Bess's poems, and how Mr. Mullaney told her they should be in the literary magazine. But what did Bess's stupid poems have to do with me?

Nothing. Absolutely nothing.

Still.

All I knew for sure was that I couldn't stand imagining

Mr. Mullaney flipping through my pointless, mindless journal, even if he wasn't going to read a single stupid word. Just the thought of him doing that made me feel like barfing.

I had to get it back. There was simply no choice.

By the time I got back to school, it was three twenty. I parked my bike without even locking it, and raced up to room 206. The door was partly open, so I walked in.

And there he was sitting at his desk, twining his long bony fingers around a steaming mug of tea. A stack of papers took up all the room on his desk. But no journals.

"Ah, Cassie," he said, looking surprised. "How may I help you?"

"I need my journal back," I said, panting. "I forgot something."

"Really? What did you forget?"

"It's too complicated," I said desperately. "Anyway, can I please just have it back?"

"I'm afraid not," he said, shaking his head.

"But *why*?"

"I brought them home at lunchtime. I have to carry things in shifts. I have a bad back, you know."

I didn't know. Or maybe I did. Because that explained

why he was moving so weirdly when he helped me find my key.

"Is there anything else I can do for you?" he asked, so quietly I thought his teeth probably hurt too. "Anything you'd like to chat about, perhaps?"

"Not really. Thanks."

"I'm always here, you know."

How pathetic. "Yeah. Well, see you tomorrow, Mr. Mullaney."

"Good-bye, then, Cassie," he said. "Don't forget: quiz tomorrow on prepositional phrases. I expect significantly better results from you this time."

"I know," I said miserably. "Bye."

And then I got back on my bike and raced home to rescue Jackson from the smoke-breathing dragon. But he didn't even say thank you; he just stomped into his room and slammed the door.

twenty-five

Four thirty. Back at my desk. Still no Miranda, still no word where she was. But she'd been in such a nasty, sulky, snotty mood this morning that it wasn't exactly surprising that she hadn't called. Of course, I had a pretty good guess where she was, anyway: probably at Madison Avenue's, eating frozen Ring Dings, waiting by the phone for that Adam person to call. Even though she was supposed to be *here,* taking care of Jackson, baking the stupid potatoes.

Monkey droppings, I thought. I was much too mad at everybody to do my Math homework, but I sort-of-did it anyway. Then I started sort-of-studying for that stupid quiz on prepositional phrases. Jackson was back in his room, stinking like cigarettes, playing Power Rangers under his blanket. The phone rang. I answered and immediately shrieked: "MIRANDA? WHERE ARE YOU?!"

"Cassie?" The voice was shocked, a little husky. Definitely not Miranda.

Yikes. I'd just sounded like a total psycho. "Yes?"

"Hi, it's Danny?"

Gulp.

"Danny?"

"Danny Abbott. From school?"

"Oh. Hi." *(Cassie, get a grip!)*

"Hi. Um, can I get the Math homework? I didn't copy it down."

"Sure. One moment." *(Cassie, you spongehead, now you sound like a receptionist!)* "Hi, Danny? It's pages one-sixteen to one-seventeen, even problems only."

"Thanks."

"You're welcome."

Now what?

"Well, bye," Danny said.

"Bye."

I hung up, kind of dizzy. He got my number, he called: That was good. I sounded like such a jerk: That was definitely bad. What just happened? And what was I supposed to *think* about what just happened? Suddenly I needed to talk to someone. Not Brianna or Hayley, that I knew. Who else, then? Miranda? No. No way. She'd tease my head off. She'd never let me alone. Besides, she'd feel—what's that word? Vindicated. She'd feel vindicated. She'd think I was turning out to be just like her: not a gifted writer—probably a novelist, with a journal—but just another Styrofoam-headed girly-girl all excited because some boy called. She'd love it. She'd be thrilled.

I couldn't let her have that satisfaction. No, not Miranda. Definitely not Miranda.

Mom, then? Sure. But when? When she came in the door exhausted from work, and all she wanted was a hug and a cup of tea and to sit on the sofa and stare at CNN?

So, who else?

Dad? Dream on, Cassie.

Bess? Maybe.

Probably.

"Cassie? Can I tell you something?" Jackson was standing at my desk.

"Yeah. What."

"When's Miranda coming home?"

"That's it? That's what you have to *tell* me?"

He blinked. "Yeah."

"That's a *question*, not a *statement*, Jackie. You don't *tell* someone a *question*."

"Oh. Sorry."

I glared at him. Spider-Man sweatshirt with a yellow paint stain, probably from "Art." Scruffy blond hair sticking up again. Booger in left nostril. Why wasn't this kid ever cleaner-looking? And on top of everything, now he stank like cigarettes.

"Why do you want Miranda?" I challenged him.

"Because I'm hungry?"

"Is *that* a question?"

"No. I'm really hungry."

"How can you be hungry? You had brownies at Mrs. Patella's."

"I didn't eat very many. They were burnt."

"Well, poor you."

"Cassie? Can I tell you something?"

"*What?*"

"Are you mad at me?"

At this point I didn't know whether to strangle Jackson or hug him. Instead I reached out and messed his weird hair. "No, Jackie. I'm not. I'm just incredibly busy right now."

"When's Miranda coming home?"

"Don't know. In a little while."

"Where is she?"

"Don't know. I'll call her friend." I sighed and dialed Madison's number, which by now I'd memorized. I was already gritting my teeth, getting ready for when Miranda got on the phone and acted all snotty, like it was all my fault she'd been grounded in the first place.

But there was no answer. That was weird. Before when I called, Madison Avenue had answered the phone on the first ring, then acted real casual. Now the phone was ringing and ringing. Where were they?

"Where's Miranda?" Jackson repeated.

"Jackson, you've got to quit asking the same questions over and over!" I snapped. "I told you, I don't know!"

Jackson stuck out his lower lip, then stomped away to his bedroom, slamming the door.

Nice going, Cassie.

But now I had to think. It was almost five, when Mom usually called to check in. What should I say when she called? That Miranda wasn't here? That she never even bothered to call to say where she was or when she'd show up? Yeah, right—I could just imagine Miranda's reaction if I said *that.* But what choice did I have? How could I cover up for Miranda if she wasn't even telling me where she was? And more important, *why* should I cover up for her, when she blamed me anyway, no matter what? Even if I lied for her, even if I cooked for her, even if I watched Jackson for her, day after stupid day?

I had one other thought. Maybe Miranda's wish had come true and she was hanging out, "studying Chem," with this Adam person. She wasn't at Madison's, so where else could she be? She never mentioned anybody else, just Madison and Adam, Madison and Adam, blah blah blah. Maybe she was at Adam's house, eating Ring Dings. It was worth a try.

I went to her desk. You'd think I'd have noticed by now, but somehow it shocked me to realize it was the complete opposite of mine. Everything was tidy, perfect, organized, with five stacks of folders clearly labeled ("Math," "Chem," "U.S. Hist," "Eng," "Span") and rainbow-colored Post-its stuck to every single piece of paper ("Due Tmrw!" "Due 2 Days!" "Due 3 Days!" "Long Term!"). She had three blue gel pens, two highlighters, five sharpened pencils, and two bottles of Wite-Out all stuck in a freakishly ugly mug we got in the gift shop at Disneyland. She had two white Beanie Baby kittens curled up on her desk like mascots (which struck me as incredibly hypocritical, considering how she neglected our *real* cats). And everything smelled sweet and kind of bathroomy, like her desk was dusted in flowery powder, the cheap kind they sold at CVS.

Miranda's desk made me want to barf. I scanned her hutch. All her books were lined up side by side, even books she hadn't read in, like, eight years (The Baby-sitters Club, Sweet Valley High). This killed me. How could Miranda's desk be so neat, so insanely organized, when she couldn't even remember to set her alarm clock or buy the stupid cat food? How could such a lazy, sloppy, irresponsible person take such good care of her own things?

Then I spotted what I was looking for: her Emerson High School directory. It was standing upright, slightly open. I grabbed it. Something fell out: a box of Merits, half-empty. Gross. So, lovely Miranda was now smoking cigarettes, stashing boxes in her powdery, perfect desk. How could she be so stupid? Did she really want to stink like Mrs. Patella? And was I supposed to cover this up for her too?

I flipped open the directory. What was Adam's last name? Did she ever mention it? Maybe not. But then I remembered the smiley-faced note, with the P.S. about Adam calling. I ran into my room, which was its usual disaster, papers and books and random thingies everywhere, and wadded-up garbage poking out of the trash can. Good thing I didn't believe in emptying the trash! There at the bottom, stuck to a dry wad of Juicy Fruit, was Miranda's old note:

Cass:

I'm at Madison's studying Chem for test tmrw. Be back at 6 (STILL YOUR TURN TO COOK!!!!!). Don't worry, I went shopping!!!!!

Be good,
Randa :)

P.S. If Adam Klein calls, PLEASE call me at Mad's: 555-0198. Thanx!!!!!

Okay, so Prince Charming was named Adam Klein. I flipped open to *K* in the directory. There he was: 555-2735. I raced back to the phone and dialed.

"Yeah?" this guy answered, as if he was just napping.

"Um, is this Adam Klein?"

"Yeah?"

"Hi, my name is Cassie Baldwin. I was wondering if maybe my sister, Miranda, was at your house. It's kind of an emergency."

"Who?"

"Miranda. Miranda Baldwin."

He paused. Maybe to think, maybe to wake up. "Miranda?"

"Yes, Miranda Baldwin. She's not at your house?"

"No. Why should she be? Did she *say* she'd be here?" All of a sudden his voice sounded different, like he thought something was really amusing. I was starting to think I'd made a big mistake by calling.

"Well, no. Okay, sorry to bother you," I squeaked. "Bye."

I hung up wincing. Yikes. If Miranda ever found out I'd called Adam, she'd probably vaporize me. But of course, I told myself quickly, it was all her own stupid fault, anyway. If only she'd told me where she was, then I wouldn't have had to call him.

Right? Right?

twenty-six

Jackson was still holed up in his room when Mom called at five thirty. "Cassie, I need to speak to you. I'll be home at seven," she said, in this all-business sort of voice.

"What's up?" I asked. "Is something wrong?"

"We'll discuss it when I get home. Where's Miranda?"

"In the kitchen," I said, lying.

"Jackson's okay?"

"Yeah, he's in his room." Not lying.

"Well, okay, then. I'd better get back to work if I'm going to catch my train. We'll talk when I get home." Then she hung up.

"Was that Miranda?" asked Jackson, standing in his doorway.

"No, just Mom," I said. "She'll be home soon."

"For supper?"

"No, later than that."

"Then who's making supper?"

I sighed. "I don't know. Me, I guess."

Jackson stuck out his lower lip. "Where's Miranda? I thought you said you were calling her friend."

"I did call her friend. I called two of her friends. I don't know where she is!"

"Call Mrs. Patella."

"Jackie, what good would that do? Mrs. Patella doesn't know where Miranda is."

"I know that! But maybe she can make us supper!"

I snorted. Just the thought of any food cooked by Mrs. Patella, the Walking Ashtray, made me want to barf. "Ah, c'mon, Jackie boy. You think I can't bake us some stupid potatoes? What am I, helpless?"

I went into the kitchen. Jackie followed. "Set the oven," he instructed.

"I know what to do!" I snapped. Sheesh, this kid could really get on your nerves sometimes. Five hundred degrees. That should cook just about anything.

"What about the hamburgers? Mom said we were having hamburgers for supper," Jackson reminded me.

"I know, I know, I know!" I opened the fridge. There

were three patties, all set to go. "Okay now, Jackie, first we have to wait for the oven to heat up, then we cook the potatoes, *then* we make the hamburgers." I liked how I sounded: totally in control.

Jackson didn't argue. All of a sudden he switched gears. "Can I watch Cartoon Network?"

"The TV's still buzzing, but sure." Anything to get him out of the kitchen.

I sat him down in front of the TV, which was now sounding like a whole *hive* of bugs. Pretty soon we'd have to wear beekeeper helmets just to watch the news. The thought of Miranda wearing a beekeeper helmet while she ate Doritos and watched MTV made me laugh in my head. Then suddenly I realized that I hadn't returned the Emerson High directory to Miranda's bathroomy desk. If she saw her cigarette pack all exposed on her hutch, she'd know that

(A) I knew she smoked cigarettes (blech!)

and

(B) For some strange reason I had her directory.

A wasn't so bad. In fact, it could work to my advantage, especially if she knew I hadn't told Mom when I clearly *could* have. But there was no way of explaining *B.* And judging by that Adam person's reaction to my call, this "relationship" she sat by the phone dreaming about was entirely in her own head. *Poor Miranda,* I thought, suddenly feeling sorry for her, for some weird reason. But then I remembered why I'd needed to call Adam in the first place, and I just got mad at her all over again. Where was she, anyway?

I put the directory back on Miranda's hutch, carefully hiding the Merits in the middle, then went back to my own nonpowdery desk. I sat down, still feeling jumpy about the Journal Fiasco. Maybe even jumpier, after talking to Danny, and then to that Adam person. And of course to Mom: What did she need to come home to talk to me about? Why did she sound so serious? Whatever this was about, it wasn't good, that much I knew.

I re-scrunchied my ponytail. Then I uncapped my black extra-fine-point Rolling Writer. Then I re-capped it. Then I uncapped it again. Suddenly I felt like writing in my journal, but, of course, tonight Sir Mullvo was clutching it in his evil talons, maliciously counting pages. And anyway, even if I had it right now, what would I write about? More pointless no-brain nonsense? More virtual tours of my insanely messy desk? More lists of funny words and HAHAHAHAHAs? To tell you the truth, what I really, really felt like writing was more of my Cat story, but by now I couldn't even remember where it ended. Since I'd gotten my "12," I hadn't looked at it, hadn't edited it, hadn't thought about it. What if I couldn't just pick up where I'd left off? What if I lost the feeling for it, the momentum? What if my story was ruined, what if it was just gone?

Maybe Bess was right that day in the cafeteria. Maybe if I stopped writing what I really cared about, Sir Mullvo had won.

I sighed a big sigh, a Miranda sigh. And when I inhaled, something definitely smelled weird.

twenty-seven

"Cassie?" Jackson was standing at my door, his eyes wide. "Can I tell you something? I think something's wrong in the kitchen."

I shot out of my room. Smoke was coming into the hallway. Weird-smelling smoke.

"Jackson, run and tell Mrs. Patella. Right now!" I pushed him out the door.

I ran into the kitchen. Black smoke was pouring out of the oven. I turned the oven switch to off, then yanked open the windows. The smoke detector started screaming anyway.

A second later, who should walk in the kitchen but Miranda. *"WHERE'S THE FIRE EXTINGUISHER?"* she hollered over the smoke detector's screams.

"Under the sink," I said. "But there's no fire!"

"THERE'S SMOKE!" she thundered. *"GET IT!"*

So I hauled it out of the cabinet under the sink and thrust it at her. She aimed it at the stove. She looked fierce, like Cat aiming her dragonfire arrow at the Mystyck Beast. She yanked something, and then white foam shot out, sudsing up the oven like a big crazy bubble bath.

"NOW TURN OFF THAT SMOKE DETECTOR!" she yelled.

I stood on a chair and pulled out the battery. The screaming stopped, but the air was still vibrating when Mrs. Patella ran in. "What happened?" she cried.

"Nothing," I said. "I was just heating up the oven. Then it got smoky."

"You were just heating up the oven?" She furrowed her brow. "How could this happen if you were just heating up the oven?"

"I don't know."

"What temperature did you set?"

"Five hundred, but—"

"*Five hundred?* What in the world were you making?"

"Baked potatoes."

"Five hundred for *baked potatoes*? Why did you set the oven so high?"

Good question. I decided to ignore it. "The oven hasn't been cleaned in a while. Maybe it was greasy or something."

Mrs. Patella perched herself on a chair. "Why were you baking potatoes?"

"For supper," I said. I flashed Miranda a look. *Help me,* I mouthed.

"Do you always do the cooking?"

"No, she doesn't," Miranda said firmly. "I do. But I wasn't here."

"I'm well aware of that. Where were you?" Mrs. Patella demanded, staring accusingly at Miranda.

"Out," she said. "Well, thanks for coming over, Mrs. Patella, but everything is just fine now, and Mom's on her way home, so we really need to clean up this mess." Then she opened the door, and even Mrs. Patella could tell that she was being kicked out.

She got up from her chair. "Call me if you need anything, girls." She frowned, then left.

"Yeah, like if we desperately need to be interrogated," Miranda snorted. "Hand me those paper towels, Cassie."

We both started cleaning up the sudsy mess. By now so much fresh air was blowing into the kitchen that it was practically freezing. But we were working so hard to dry up the oven and the floor that it actually felt pretty good.

After a while I broke the silence. "How did you know Mom was on her way home?" I asked Miranda.

"I didn't. She is?"

"I wanted to warn you, but I didn't know where you were."

She didn't answer.

"Mom asked where you were," I said.

She stopped cleaning. "Oh? And what did you say?"

"I said you were here."

She tossed a sudsy wad of paper towel into the trash. Then she sighed. "Well, you certainly got me into big trouble now," she said.

"What?"

"Mrs. Patella knows I was out. She'll tell Mom."

"Maybe, Miranda. But if she does, that's not *my* fault! I was trying to cover up for you."

"Yeah? Well, thanks, but I guess you're in trouble too, then."

I stared at Miranda in disbelief, but almost immediately realized she was right. Of course Mrs. Patella would tell Mom that I was the one incinerating the potatoes. Of course

Mom would know that (a) Miranda wasn't here, and (b) I lied to her about it. Of course Mrs. Patella would tell her that I frantically ran out of the house to go back to school for some mysterious "special project," leaving her to babysit for Jackson. But if Miranda had been here, like she was *supposed* to be, I could have gone back to school, and Mom wouldn't even have had to know. It wasn't fair, none of it!

"Cassie? Miranda?" Jackson was standing in the kitchen in his bare feet. "What are you doing?"

"What does it look like, goofball?" Miranda grinned. "Get over here and give me a big hug."

Jackson did. Why was he always so glad to see her when she was such a rotten big sister?

"I'm hungry," he announced. Sheesh. It was like his theme song.

"Me too," Miranda said. "Tell you what. I'll order in some pizza. My treat."

I stared at her. "But Mom told you to make hamburgers, remember?"

"Of course I remember. But let's just give the kitchen a rest now, okay, Cass? Anyhow, I have a feeling it's going to be a long night once Mom gets home, so let's just treat ourselves, okay?"

About an hour later Mom walked in the door. The kitchen was spotless, and the air was still chilly. Mom stood in the kitchen for a few seconds, hands on her hips, not saying anything, but definitely sniffing the air once or twice. Then she looked at me with laser-beam eyes.

"All right, Cassie," she said. "Let's talk."

twenty-eight

We sat down at the table. Mom took off her coat. "Miranda and Jackson, please go to your rooms," she said.

That set me off. "So, I'm in trouble and Miranda isn't?"

Mom smiled grimly. "You first."

They left the kitchen. I looked at Miranda to see if maybe she was celebrating, because I was the one in trouble for a change, not all wrapped up in my—what did she call it? My perfect little planet. But instead of grinning evilly, she mouthed *Good luck* and gave a quick thumbs-up. That was certainly weird.

Mom clasped her hands and leaned forward. I could smell her work perfume, which was different from her weekend perfume. More serious, somehow. "Cassie, I can't conceal my disappointment," she said. "I've always expected such good judgment from you, but I'm so upset right now, I barely know where to start."

I stared at her. Maybe this wasn't about Miranda, or the stupid baked potatoes, after all.

"I spoke to Jackson's teacher today," she said. "First of all, did you write a book report for him about Farmer Joe?"

I snorted. "Yes, I did. But, Mom, it was a completely stupid assignment! You weren't home, Jackson was all upset, I tried to help him, but he didn't have any ideas. None! He could barely read the stupid book, so how was he supposed to write a report? So I dictated something a little silly, so maybe his teacher would pay some attention to him."

Mom looked shocked. "Mrs. Rivera? Not paying attention? What are you *talking* about?"

"But Jackie said—" Then I stopped. What *had* Jackson said, exactly? That his teacher sounded out words with him "maybe once"? Or that he just *remembered* his teacher sounding out words with him "maybe once"? Jackson wasn't always so clear about things, I had to admit.

But Mom wasn't waiting for me to figure this out. "Mrs. Rivera is paying a huge amount of attention to him, Cassie. She has him in a special reading group, she gives him special books and projects, she talks to me on the phone every week about his progress. I couldn't ask for a better, more devoted teacher. So you can just imagine how horrified, how embarrassed, I was when she called to tell me that Jackson turned in a book report calling Farmer Joe a 'total psycho'!"

I winced. "Mom, it was supposed to be funny."

"Well, Mrs. Rivera wasn't amused. *At all.* I know you have a great sense of humor, Cassie, but whatever it was you dictated was entirely inappropriate. And then, Cassie, she said you told her that I wanted Jackson tested for a *learning disability*?"

I swallowed. "Yes, but—"

"Yes, but what?"

I sighed. "I tried to talk to you about it. I tried Miranda, too. But you both just acted like it was no big deal, like it was normal that Jackson couldn't read or write and was crying all the time."

"Cassie, I told you, not every kid is as precocious as you were. Lots of kids struggle in first grade, and it's not because they have a learning disability."

"Yes, Mom, okay, but he should at least be *starting* to read. He isn't! Do you even know this?"

Mom looked really, really angry. Her eyebrows shot up, and her brown eyes flashed. "Cassandra. Watch what you're saying. Of *course* I know this. I read with him every single chance I get. Even when I come home from work after a long, stressful day and all I want is to crawl into bed, I sit with him and practice word lists and play alphabet bingo. And yes, *of course* I wish I had more time to work with him. Of course I wish I was around more. But you're old enough to understand that somebody in this family has to be out earning a paycheck. So don't go blaming me for Jackie's problems with reading!"

"No, Mom, listen! I know it's not your fault that you aren't here. It's not anybody's fault. Not even Dad's."

She flinched. "We're not talking about Dad right now."

"Okay, fine. We won't discuss Dad. We'll never, ever discuss Dad, if that's really what you want!"

"Don't say that, Cassie," she murmured, shaking her head. "It isn't fair."

"You mean it isn't fair *to you*?"

"I mean, it isn't fair to anyone."

"But why?"

She paused. "Because Dad should talk to you himself.

He has something very difficult to say, and he should be the one to say it."

"Fine! Great! So when will that be, exactly?"

"I don't know, honey. I wish I could give you an exact day and time, but it isn't in my control. You understand that, right?"

I gave a half-nod, which meant my head went down but didn't come back up.

"Look at me, Cassie," she said. "It's going to happen. It's awful not knowing when; I feel as terrible about that as you, but all I can promise is, it will definitely happen. Sometime soon."

"This week? This millennium?"

"I don't have a specific date. Just soon."

"But how can you promise if you don't even know anything?"

"Because Dad told me he would, and I believe that," she said very quietly. "Sometimes you just have to believe things, Cassie."

Neither of us said anything. The kitchen clock sounded like a magician flipping over cards: *Was it this one? Was it this?* Finally I took a sharp breath. "So, what's going to happen, Mom? I mean, with you and Dad. Are you getting a divorce?"

"I really can't talk about that," she answered automatically. There must have been an insane expression on my face, because she added, "Nothing's settled. I don't know anything for sure right now. But—well, probably we will be, honey, yes."

She sank back into her chair then, pale and limp, as if a dragonfire arrow had pierced her heart. My dragonfire arrow. I wanted to hug her, I wanted to tell her everything would be okay, but I was definitely at war, and I wasn't finished. I took another breath.

"Listen, Mom, I'm not blaming you. For anything. Really! I know how hard you're working. I know how tired you are when you get home."

"Well, thank you."

"But the truth is, Jackson isn't getting enough attention, and I had to do something."

She sat up a little straighter now. "So you lied to Mrs. Rivera. You told her I said something I never said. We spent two days trading phone calls just to iron it out."

I didn't answer.

"You lied. And when I called you today and asked where Miranda was, you lied about that, too, didn't you?"

"That's a completely different thing!"

"Is it?"

"Yes! I was just trying to help Miranda. I didn't know where she was, and I didn't want to get her in trouble."

"Really? You lied to protect her? *Why?*"

"I don't know. You were at work. I didn't want you to worry."

She shook her head. I could see the color creeping back into her cheeks. "Cassie, I'm really shocked by your bad judgment. If Mrs. Patella hadn't called me at work, I wouldn't have known that Miranda wasn't here, or that we almost had a fire, isn't that right?"

My throat was getting tight. *Cassie, whatever you do, don't cry.* "It wasn't a fire, it was just a smoky oven! And you're so busy, Mom, you have other things to worry about. I was only trying to protect you."

"Protect me? From what? Listen, Cassie, I'm the mother around here, you're the kid, and it's *my* job to protect *you.*" Then she reached across the table to touch my arm. "I may not be here very much, but that's exactly why I need to know what's going on."

I looked at the table. There were two Cheerios left over from breakfast. I squashed them with my index finger. "Okay," I said.

She let out some air. "Good, then. So? Is there anything else I don't know about? While we're on the subject? Anything about school, for example?"

I poked the Cheerios dust. Was this a trick question? Did she know something about the journal? Had Sir Mullvo called her about my trips to fantasyland, like he'd threatened to?

I swallowed hard. "No," I said. Lying.

"All right. From now on, I'm going to ask Mrs. Patella to check in with you kids every day after school. Just to make sure everyone's accounted for."

"Oh, great," I said. "Miranda's going to love *that*."

"I'll deal with Miranda," Mom said firmly. "And as for you, Cassie, I'm sure you understand that I need to give you a punishment. I wish I didn't, but this is really serious, so I'm grounding you for a month. Maybe you can use the time to work with Jackson on his reading."

I stared at her in disbelief. "You're grounding me? For what? Trying to help Miranda? Sticking up for Jackson?"

"For lying. To Mrs. Rivera and to me. Listen, Cassie. I understand that you did what you thought was right. You actually thought you were taking care of everyone—Jackson, Miranda, somehow, in some strange way I still don't understand, even me. But nothing is worse than lying, sweetheart."

That "sweetheart" thing just did it. I knew if I sat there any longer I would burst into tears, which I definitely didn't want to do. So I ran into my room and slammed my door and started punching my pillows. And yes, it was incredibly babyish of me, but I was just so furious and humiliated and exhausted. After this long, long day, it seemed incredible that I was the one being punished. And for what? For defending everyone. For thinking about their feelings. For being responsible. For being *here*. And how was I being punished? By being *grounded*, when the truth was that I was grounded anyway, every single day of my stupid life.

A few minutes later it was Miranda's turn to get yelled at. I couldn't hear very much—just an occasional "selfish" and "serious." By the time they finished I was 98 percent asleep, curled up in bed with Buster and Fuzzy, the best, and maybe the only, friends I had on the planet. Which, incidentally, was light years away from perfect.

twenty-nine

At breakfast the next morning I was still so mad I couldn't talk. Mom and Miranda kept trying to catch my eye, but I refused to look at either of them. As far as I was concerned they were equally guilty: Miranda for going "out" and forcing me to lie for her, and Mom for completely missing the point of my whole existence. How could she ground me? What sense did it make? It was what you did to someone who actually had privileges worth taking away. Only what privileges, what freedom, did I have, thanks to Miranda, who could just go "out" all the time and smoke stupid cigarettes and not buy cat food, while I had to stay behind in the ratty little "unit" to write book reports for Jackson and burn potatoes.

Not only that, but the whole idea of being grounded made me want to barf. It was such a teenage word:

"grounded." No trips to the mall, no Saturday-night dates for you, Muffy, because you're *grounded.* Mom (or Dad, for that matter) had never grounded me before in my whole life. I mean, I remember a long time-out once for poking Miranda with a chopstick in a Chinese restaurant. And when I was eight, I didn't get my allowance for three weeks (when we got allowances, before Dad was "out of the picture") because I cut the hair off my cousin Nell's Barbie. But this was the first time I'd been punished in centuries, and how was Mom doing it? By *grounding* me, like I was this careless, selfish, misbehaving teenager. Like I was Miranda. It was disgusting.

I went to school in the worst mood possible.

And when I got there, three terrible things happened.

First: The strap of my backpack broke, so I had to carry it in my arms like a big fat squirming baby.

Second: Lindsay Frost decided to have a bowling party on Saturday night, and invited the whole class. Not just the cool kids like Brianna and Hayley and Danny and Noah—but everyone, including the groupless losers, including people like Zachary Hairball and Bess Waterbury.

Oh yeah. And including me.

Only I couldn't go. And why? Because I was *grounded.*

Third: At the very end of fourth period English, Sir Mullvo handed back the journals. Didn't say a word, didn't announce my page total to the class. Did, however, write this on the inside cover:

Cassie Baldwin:
63 pages.
See me during next lunch period.

See him? See him do what? Combat scurvy? Lance a repulsive pustule? Kiss a slobbering ogress? Why in the world would I want to *see Mr. Mullaney*?

So, the following period, when it was time for lunch, I grabbed a pretzel in the lunchroom, then hid out in the library. Way in the back near the *National Geographic* magazines, where nobody ever went.

I unzipped my squirming backpack baby and took out my journal. Then I flipped back sixty-three pages. Where had I left off my Cat story? Oh, right: Cat was giving Daeman target practice, and the lovely Gloriana was shrieking her head off. Just another fun-filled day in fantasyland, I guess.

I uncapped my black extra-fine-point Rolling Writer. Then I wrote.

Cat carefully packed her three precious arrows in her (whatchamacallit), then laced her riding boots.

"Cat! Where are you going?" cried Daeman.

"Out to slay beasts," Cat replied. "My work here is done."

"What are you talking about?"

"Sorry, Daeman. But I can't just sit here with you day after day shooting feather pillows."

"But the Queen told you to!"

"Yes. But this is not the best use of my Gift. I need to get out there in the kingdom and fight. The King is counting on me to hold the fort."

"But the Queen punished you for letting Valdyk go, remember?"

"Of course I remember, Daeman! It's a mistake I regret, believe me. And I can't promise you I won't make the same mistake a second time. But I need to get out there and look right into his evil eyes! I can't just sit around in the castle forever!"

"But Cat! The Queen needs you!"

"I know. But she needs me to fight for her, not to waste my Gift." Cat's little cousin began to cry. "Don't worry, Daeman. Cheer up. You'll be just fine."

Okay, so I was a bit rusty. But it sure felt good to be writing something meaningful, something important (well, at least to me), even if it didn't fill up the right number of pages, even if it didn't get an A. Yes, even if I was the only one who would ever actually read it. And when the bell rang, and it was time for Math, I carried my fat, squirming backpack baby down the hall, not even caring how pathetic I looked, or that I was sure to be in even worse trouble when I got home.

thirty

"Cassie? There was a *male caller,*" Miranda teased as I dumped my backpack baby on the kitchen table.

I froze; I forgot to be mad at her. "Did he ask to talk to Mom?"

She snorted. "No, goofball! To you."

"Mr. Mullaney wanted to talk to *me*?"

Now she laughed. "Mr. Mullaney? Where did you get that? No, Casshead, some *boy* called. Danny Abbott?"

"Oh."

"*Oh?* What, don't you like him?"

"No, I do." Immediately I felt like kicking myself. Telling Miranda was *not* what I'd planned.

Weirdly, though, she didn't seem surprised. "So, what's he like?" she asked.

"I don't know. Cute. Sort of." I sat down. "Did he leave a message?"

"Nope. He said he'll call back."

I sank into the kitchen chair. Then I closed my eyes.

"Cassie, what's wrong? You look terrible."

I don't know why, but there was something about the way Miranda looked at me just then that made me want to talk to her. Something in her eyes, maybe. Whatever it was, I opened my mouth and started telling her *everything.* Not just about how I couldn't go to Lindsay's stupid bowling party and how dorky I felt all day because of my stupid backpack. But also the big stuff: about Mr. Mullaney, and my Cat story, and the whole pointless page-counting journal. Then I told her about how I hid out in the library instead of "seeing" Mr. Mullaney when he gave it back, and how I was positive he would report me to the principal or, even worse, call Mom.

Miranda didn't say anything. She just listened. Then she shocked me.

"You have to tell Mom," she said.

"WHAT?"

"Listen, Cassie, I mean it. After all that's happened since yesterday, if you don't tell Mom about Mr. Mullaney and he calls here, and it sounds like he definitely will, she'll never trust you again. And believe me, if you think being grounded for a month is bad, that would be a whole lot worse."

I sighed. "Yeah. You're right, I guess. But first I'm going to call Danny back."

"*Why?* No, no, Cassie, let *him* call *you.*"

This was such an insanely Miranda thing to say that I actually laughed, despite how miserable I felt. "Oh, come on, Ran. He probably just wants the Math homework."

She got up. "Whatever," she said, leaving the kitchen.

So I checked the Emerson Middle School directory for Danny's number, then dialed. As I was punching in the numbers, it occurred to me that Adam Klein probably hadn't said anything to Miranda about my phone call yesterday. If he had, she'd have been psycho just now, not all sympathetic and actually *nice.* Phew. It was like I'd dodged a poisoned arrow.

"Hello?"

"Hi, Danny? It's Cassie. You called just now?"

"Uh, yeah." He sounded confused, kind of like how Adam sounded. Did all boys fall asleep next to the phone?

"Yeah," he repeated. "So, uh, Cassie? Are you going to that bowling party on Saturday?"

Was this why he called? Not about the Math homework?

"I can't, actually. I would but I'm grounded."

"Oh."

Pause.

"Well, too bad. See you," he said quickly, then hung up.

I hung up too, and just stood there.

"So? He wanted the Math homework?" Miranda asked, strolling into the kitchen as if she just happened to be in the neighborhood.

"No," I said. Then I realized I was grinning. "I think he just sort of asked me out."

Her eyebrows shot up. "Way to go, Cassandra! What did you tell him?"

"That I couldn't, because I'm grounded. That it's all your fault."

She opened her mouth as if she were about to start yelling.

"Only kidding," I said, sticking out my tongue.

She laughed. It was such a nice laugh, giggly but not too giggly, friendly but also siblingy, that before I knew what I was doing, I blurted out: "ListenMirandaIcalledAdamKlein!"

"You what?"

"Yesterday, when you didn't come home, I tried Madison's, but you weren't there. So I called his house; I got the number from the directory. I'm really, really sorry, Miranda, so please don't kill me!"

She stared at me, vibrating a little. "You called his *house?*"

I nodded.

"And what did he say?"

"Not much. That you weren't there, either."

All of a sudden Miranda threw her arms around me. "Cassie, you're a genius!"

"I am?"

"Of course you are, you idiot! Thank you, thank you, THANK YOU!"

She gave me an ecstatic squeeze, which I totally did *not* understand, and then two seconds later she pulled away. "So? Are you going to call Mom about this teacher thing?"

It was very strange. Maybe it was because of how Miranda spared my life, or maybe it was because of Danny sort-of-asking me out. But it occurred to me right then that I was feeling a zillion times better about the whole Sir Mullvo business. "I'll tell her, Ran. But first I'm going to try to take care of it. Myself."

She gave a big dramatic shrug. "Your funeral," she said.

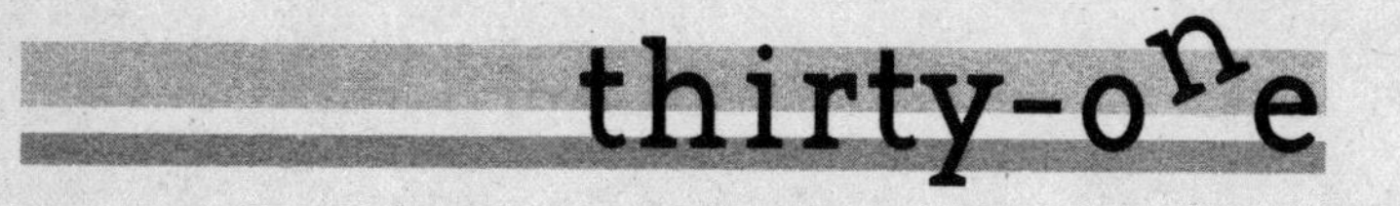

thirty-one

The next day I showed up at school with my backpack duct-taped ("Nice look," Brianna smirked), happy about Danny (but avoiding eye contact), and nervous about Sir Mullvo (but ready to do battle). English was last period today, which meant that first I had to get through: a pop quiz in Science, another team-drawing exercise in Art, a long boring video in Social Studies, volleyball in Gym, I don't remember what in Health, more fun with fractions in Math. Oh yeah, and at lunch, turkey burgers that looked like cat barf. I made myself another gloppy yogurt sundae and sat down with Bess.

"Sorry I wasn't here yesterday," I apologized. "I went to the library. To work on my novel."

She looked up from her fruit salad. "Yeah? The fantasy one?"

"Yeah. I've decided to keep writing it. You were right. I couldn't let Mr. Mullaney win," I said.

She grinned. "Good. Can I see it sometime?"

"Sure. Not yet, though. I'm still deciding how it should come out."

"When it's ready," she said. "And maybe I'll show you mine. But it's really not that good," she added quickly.

I grinned back at her. "Don't worry," I said. "I won't even count the pages."

Finally it was time for English. Mr. Mullaney was going on and on about some stupid story in the so-called "fiction textbook" he kept handing out to us, only I'd lost the third page of it because it wasn't even stapled together. What was the point of taking notes on a stupid story you couldn't even read? So I quietly slipped out my journal and began writing.

Cat's horse Starlight cantered purposefully to Valdyk's iron gate. "Stay calm, Cat," she told herself. "Stay focused."

Starlight reared as she approached the gate, as if she sensed something bad was about to happen. Cat patted her, dismounted slowly, then turned to the building up ahead. Valdyk's castle. She'd know it anywhere.

She silently entered the Main Chamber, which was strangely empty. Where was everybody? Where were the sentinels? Where were the bodyguards? And where was Valdyk?

"Ah, my lovely Catrain, so it's finally you," a voice sneered.

Cat spun around, her green eyes flashing.

"I see you've decided to do something meaningful, after all," he said. "Welcome to my world."

"Hello, Sir Mullvo," Cat replied calmly. "I had a feeling I'd find you here. I had a feeling all along."

The bell rang. Everyone raced out to get to their lockers before the bus, but I stayed behind, pretending to pack my duct-taped backpack very slowly and carefully, like it had just had lifesaving surgery. Brianna called out, "Hurry up, Cassie, you don't want to be late for your bicycle," and Hayley giggled like that was the wittiest remark in the history of the English language. But I just waggled my fingers at them in a kind of Hollywood way, then walked up to Mr. Mullaney's desk.

"Can I talk to you," I *said*, not *asked*. "About my journal."

He straightened his mouth. "I've been waiting for you," he sneered. He got up to shut the door.

"Sixty-three," I said. "Pretty good, huh?"

He made a face like he was eating a repulsive pustule. "Pretty bad, actually. Yes, you filled your journal with lots of pages, but all of it was empty-headed nonsense. You're the best writer in the class. I expect a great deal more from you, Cassie."

What?

My legs felt funny, all of a sudden. I sat down.

"So you actually read it?" I asked.

"Of course I read it. Do you think I'd assign some writing and then not actually read it?"

"But you didn't read my novel!"

"Wherever did you get that idea?"

"All you wrote was a '12'. You just counted the pages."

He clasped his bony fingers. "Yes. That's right. I did count the pages. If I didn't count the pages, there are students who would just hand in a paragraph and feel they'd satisfied the assignment. The page requirement is just to get the class to develop their pieces, to keep writing, to keep working."

"But you didn't say anything else about my story," I said in a strangled voice. "You just gave it a page number."

"No. You're right. I didn't write anything else. But that's because it isn't my place to comment on your creative work. The journal is supposed to be for you, not for me, Cassie. I don't want you to write your story for a grade or a comment. I want you to write it for yourself."

"Yeah, well, you commented on Bess's poems!"

"Perhaps I did," he admitted. "But we're not discussing Bess, are we."

My head swam. This conversation was the complete opposite of what I'd expected. One hundred eighty degrees. I sat there, totally not knowing what to say.

"All right, Cassie. If you insist on a comment, here it is," he said finally. "Some of your story was really rather clever. Some of it, and let's not specify which sections, I thought was rather—how shall I put it? *Uncharitable.* A certain character, and let's not specify which one, was a pretty mean-spirited *caricature.* But on the whole it was an excellent first effort, full of spirit, and showed a real appreciation of the fantasy genre."

He paused. Then he looked right into my face. When he spoke again, his voice sounded quieter, like his teeth ached and it hurt to talk. "A lot of what you wrote *this* time was simply hostile. Occasionally amusing in a juvenile way, but hostile. What it told me, Cassie, more than anything else, is that you are seriously craving attention."

"What?"

"I think you heard what I said. You're too bright to play dumb."

"Well, I'm not playing dumb, Mr. Mullaney, and I'm not craving attention, either!"

"Excuse me, but I think you are, so let me repeat my offer to you, Cassie: *I am always here.* If you'd ever like help with your novel, or with prepositional phrases, or finding your bicycle key, anything at all, you know exactly where to find me."

I stared at him, *outraged* that he was saying this, when all I really wanted was for him to say my stuff should be in the literary magazine, like Bess's stupid, pathetic little poems. My mouth was hanging open; I was so insulted with his offer of "help" that I couldn't even talk.

And then it started.

I don't know why, but suddenly all of the crying that I

hadn't done for months just came bursting out. First it was furious tears, then humiliated tears, then missing-Dad tears, then just tears-tears. I couldn't stop it; it just kept coming out of me. Every time I thought it was stopping, it started up again. Pretty soon it was like the room wasn't there, and Mr. Mullaney wasn't there, and even I wasn't there.

Mr. Mullaney looked alarmed. He obviously wasn't used to dealing with sobbing, hysterical seventh-grade girls, so it took him about a minute too long to hand me a tissue. And then once he handed me the tissue, he didn't know what else to do, so he got up and got the whole box of tissues and put it in front of me. Then he got up again and brought over the wastebasket so I'd have some place to throw the tissues. Then he patted my shoulder a couple of times and just sat there watching me with a worried toothachey look on his face.

Finally the tears stopped coming and I sat there hiccupping and gasping and honking my nose.

Mr. Mullaney got up again and went into the hallway. Then he came back with a little Dixie cup full of water. "Drink it," he said, so I did.

"You're welcome to stay as long as you like," he said quietly. "I'm going to grade some papers. You can do your homework or whatever you want, and when you're ready we can call your mom to get you home."

"Mom's at work," I said, still sniffling. "And I'm ready now." I grabbed a bunch of tissues. "Okay if I take these?"

"Of course," he said. "Are you sure? I'm not going anywhere."

"I'm sure," I said, and raced out of the building to unlock my bike.

thirty-two

Of course, after all that crying I couldn't just get on my bike and go home and listen to Miranda yakking on the phone and Jackson whining about how hungry he was. I needed to be by myself; I needed time to unplug my brain and forget all about Mr. Mullaney and his stupid, infuriating, humiliating *niceness.* And also about the whole Journal Fiasco, which had turned out even worse than I'd imagined. Because now, instead of thinking that I was too clever and witty and creative to turn in pathetic book summaries and stupid haikus, Mr. Mullaney obviously thought that I was this insanely emotional baby who just *seriously craved attention.* It was all too awful to deal with, and the only thing that seemed to make any sense was moving my body, burning some energy. So I got on my bike and started to ride.

It was a damp November afternoon, and the air felt like it was psyching itself up to snow. But I didn't care; I was exhausted and sweaty from all the crying, and the cold air felt good. At first I found myself riding down Evergreen Road, past all those big fancy houses with their turrets and their saunas and their nonbuzzing TVs. And then I thought about Bess's calm blue bedroom, and all those shelves full of books. Maybe I'd knock on her door and see if I could hang out there for a while, maybe borrow something else.

So I pulled up to her driveway and got off my bike and rang her doorbell. But nobody came to the door except Rudy, who barked and barked like I was this intruder or thief or vandal or something. He was barking so loudly that I started to think all the nosy neighbors on the block could hear him. Pretty soon they'd start to think I was a criminal too, and maybe even call the police. So I got back on my bike and kept going down the street, once just barely missing some stupid little kid on a scooter.

I'd only ever been on Evergreen Road that one other time, when I visited Bess, so I wasn't exactly sure where it led, but that didn't even matter. I liked not knowing; it felt good just to ride. After a while I ended up on Sycamore

Street, which took me past the library and my orthodontist's office. I could have taken a left and been on Main Street, which would have eventually turned in to ratty old Shady Woods. Instead I took a right, which put me on Emerson Drive.

Emerson Drive was the main road of Emerson. It was the only road that was wide enough to allow trucks, and it was always noisy and full of traffic. To tell you the truth, it wasn't much fun to ride a bike on, but at this point I wasn't thinking about fun. I just wanted to keep moving; I just wanted to *travel.* I felt like if I stopped, I would have to think, and all the thoughts I could possibly have would be angry, or humiliated, or sad.

So I kept pedaling.

But of course it's impossible to have *no* thoughts for very long: Pretty soon they creep back into your head, even if you try to kick them out.

And the thought that kept creeping back into my head was this: *Maybe this is what happened to Dad.*

Maybe one day something bad happened, or not even something bad, maybe just something stupid or embarrassing, and he started moving, and he couldn't stop.

Maybe he didn't intend to go to Florida; maybe that's just where he ended up (if that's where he even was). Maybe once he got there he felt so bad about running away in the first place that he couldn't retrace his steps and just come back.

Of course, Miranda would say, *he could have called once in a while.*

Actually, he did call, Miranda. Five times, remember? Three times in August, but you kept hanging up.

Yes, I did, Miranda would say. *Because I was mad. But if he really loved us, he would have called back!*

Well, maybe he was scared to call back. Or maybe he thought it would be better for Mom to forget him, to start over with a new husband.

Okay, Miranda would say. *But that's Mom. What about his kids? What about* us*?*

I couldn't answer that.

Except to think that maybe his plan was to let some time pass and then recontact us when we were ready to give him a second chance. When we'd answer the phone without hanging up.

You're just mindlessly defending him, Cassie, Miranda would say. *You're just making up fairy tales.*

But I'm traveling too, I would answer. *See? I think I might understand just how Dad feels. Or felt.*

A big smelly truck honked its horn at me, and I swerved to the right, almost falling off my bike. My heart was pounding from all that pedaling, and the sky was getting grayer and thicker and meaner. So I decided to take the next street and get off Emerson Drive, maybe rest for a second or two to catch my breath.

Bradley Avenue, which led to the park. *Well, why not,* I thought. It was where kids *went* in Emerson. There was a lot of skateboarding there, and also a lot of standing around and laughing. Plus a lot of other stuff, I bet. Miranda told me that Emerson Park was where all the high school kids went when they went on "dates."

Not that I expected to see Danny there. Running into Danny by "accident" wasn't even remotely on my mind. First of all, it was a nasty, miserable day and nobody else would be crazy enough to be out in the park. And second of all, Danny had told me he never even rode his bike in Bradley Park. Besides, it was starting to get dark, and who would be stupid enough to be out riding at night?

Well, me. I was. And I also did it that time I went to CVS for the cat food. Of course, then I didn't have any choice; now I was choosing to do this, and it felt, well, great. Because for once in my life no one was interrupting me, or making me feed them, or yelling. And sure, I'd promised Mom I wouldn't go riding again at night, but this was different. And anyway, she was at work; she wouldn't even have to know.

So I just kept pedaling.

It was definitely better to be on normal, quiet Bradley Avenue, and pretty soon I was at the park entrance. It's funny how familiar it seemed, even though I hadn't been there since last spring. The lights were coming on, and I could see the playground area where I used to play in the sandbox when I was little, and the baseball field where Jackson had his fourth birthday party. And beyond that was a volleyball court where sometimes on a Sunday morning Dad and I would toss beachballs back and forth, cracking each other up with the worst possible knock-knock jokes.

Happy birthday, dearest Cassie
Never was a nicer lassie.

Suddenly I felt like I just couldn't ride one more minute. I got off my bike and sat down on a peeling green bench and just stared at the volleyball court, watching the leaves swirl around and around in mini-tornadoes. I wasn't even sure how much time passed; I was wearing a watch, but I hadn't checked what time I'd sat down, so what was the point of trying to figure it out? And anyway, I already knew I was pathetically late getting home. If I actually knew what time it was, I would just feel even worse. So I didn't even look.

But I was starting to get really cold now, and the wind was picking up, and I was thinking that it was probably time to leave. Maybe just a few more minutes, I told myself. And then three teenage boys I didn't recognize came skateboarding in my direction, doing those fancy skateboard moves that probably have special names.

"Hey, little girl!" one of them shouted. "Okay if we borrow your bike?"

The other two started laughing; the shouter pushed them both, and then he started laughing too.

My heart flipped over. I didn't even answer them, I just got on my bike and pedaled like crazy right out of the park.

But I didn't go home. By now it was definitely, officially dark, and I was cold and tired and hungry. But I couldn't go back to the ratty little "unit" and deal with everything there, all the yakking and fighting and buzzing. I had one more place to go, and fortunately it was right nearby.

Seven houses down from Bradley Park, just past the Langleys, was our old blue house: now painted yellow, but still definitely ours. Only Dad lost it somehow, or Mom did, or maybe both of them. From carelessness? Something *bad*? Some stupid mistake that couldn't be fixed, even though Miranda said Dad could fix just about anything, even computers and washing machines?

The house just blinked at me like a cat, not giving anything away, no matter how hard or how long I looked at it.

I'm defending you, Dad. And I'll keep on defending you. But eventually I'll want some answers, okay, Dad? OKAY?

Finally I couldn't stand there waiting any longer. I got on my bike and rode home as fast as I could, mostly just to keep from freezing.

thirty-three

When I walked into the living room about twenty minutes later, it was total mayhem.

Miranda and Jackson were there, and so was Mrs. Patella, and so was Mom. First Miranda yelled, "It's *Cassie*!" and then Jackson jumped on top of me like a ten-month-old yellow Lab, and then Mom came running over, screaming, "CASSIE, IT'S ALMOST SEVEN O'CLOCK. WHERE HAVE YOU BEEN?" Then she threw her arms around me and burst into tears.

It's a funny thing about crying. When you're doing it, you think, okay, this is just the way I feel right now. And when another kid is doing it, you think, poor kid, I wonder what's wrong. But when a grown-up is crying, it's just awkward and embarrassing, and you want to be anywhere else.

Fortunately, she didn't cry for very long. After about half a minute she let go of me and looked me up and down and demanded, "WELL?"

"You scared us out of our wits," Mrs. Patella chimed in, before I could even answer. "Lucky I was home to get Jackson when he got off the bus!"

"I was here too," Miranda reminded her. "Don't forget that!"

"WELL?" Mom repeated, not taking her eyes off me.

I sank down on the sofa. "First I had something to do at school."

"Yes, I know," Mom said, sitting down beside me and putting her arm around my shoulders. "Mr. Mullaney called me at work. He said you were very upset and he was concerned, so I came straight home."

"Yeah, well, I *was* upset, but then I was fine, but I needed to ride around for a while and clear my head."

"Even though you're grounded?" Mrs. Patella demanded.

Mom turned to her and smiled. "Listen, Rose, you've been an enormous help, and I can't thank you enough. But now that Cassie's home, I think we just need a little family time."

So Mrs. Patella was getting kicked out again. Suddenly

I felt sorry for her. But I still wanted her to leave.

Mom walked her to the door, thanked her again, and then sat back down on the sofa.

"So," I asked nervously, "am I in trouble?"

"You are with me," snapped Miranda. "Why didn't you call me from school?"

"Miranda, please," Mom said. "After all *you've* been up to, you have no right to scold Cassie. About anything!"

Miranda turned Crayola Crimson, but she didn't storm out of the room. She just shrugged and muttered, "Okay, Mom, okay."

I stared at Mom. "Then you know?"

She nodded slowly. "Well, I think I have a pretty good picture of what's been going on around here lately. It seems you've been taking care of practically everything—shopping, cooking, taking care of Jackson, helping him with his schoolwork—without tattling or complaining one little bit."

"Well, maybe one *little* bit," Miranda said, grinning.

Mom smiled, but it was a serious smile. "And I was probably way too harsh with you the other day, Cassie, and I'm sorry. But before now I just didn't understand everything you were dealing with. I really wish you'd told me!"

I swallowed hard. "Me too." Then I decided to go for it. "Does this mean I'm not grounded anymore?"

Mom shook her head. "No, sweetheart, the punishment stands, because you lied to me, and that's something I just can't ignore. But I'll overlook what happened today, because you're obviously due for a break."

It wasn't the answer I'd hoped for, but it wasn't as bad as it could have been, I guess. So all I said was, "Thanks."

She took my hand and pressed it between hers. Her hands were so warm that it made me realize how cold mine were. "Cassie, I'm just so proud of how you've coped with everything here. And on top of all that, Mr. Mullaney says you've produced the beginning of a whole novel, plus sixty-three pages of comedy writing for his class!"

SHEEPSKIN! He called it "comedy writing"? Well, at least that was better than telling her it was a cry for "serious attention," or something equally humiliating and pathetic.

"So, did he say anything about the comedy writing?" I asked, wincing a little.

"Actually, he said it was—what was his word? 'Provocative.' He said he thought you needed an audience, and that you're clever and funny and very talented. But of course, I already knew that."

She gave me a big hug. And then I needed to ask an important question, so I pulled away. "But, Mom, how exactly did you find out everything?"

"From Mrs. Patella."

"She *spied* on us?"

"Of course not. Where did you get that idea? No, she heard about it from Jackson."

"You ratted, you little monster?" I screeched, making raptor claws with my hands.

He giggled, looking like the cute little brother he used to be. "Are you mad at me, Cassie?"

"Yes! I'm so mad I'm going to eat you up!" I tickled his chest while he laughed his head off. Mom laughed too, which was good to hear.

"Of course, now *I've* been grounded for the rest of my life," Miranda complained.

"We'll discuss your situation later, Miranda," Mom said. "Right now I'm just so relieved that Cassie's home and everything's fine. Sweetheart, please don't ever take off like that without telling us where you are!"

I grinned. "Yes, Mom, I never will. I absolutely promise."

And then she ordered us a pizza to celebrate.

thirty-four

The next Friday we got our first-quarter report cards. Not surprisingly, Mr. Mullaney failed me in English. But this is what he wrote for a comment:

After conferring with Cassie I am certain that she now understands the nature and purpose of her ongoing assignments and will henceforth submit only her very best work. I daresay she will endeavor to learn the grammatical concepts explored in class, including prepositional phrases. She is a gifted writer (who/whom) is capable of great things. I look forward to awarding her the A she richly deserves.

Mom gave me a that's-very-strange look when she read this. "When I spoke with Mr. Mullaney on the phone last week, he had nothing but praise for you. In fact, he told me you're the best writer in the class. So how could he possibly fail you?"

"I made a big mistake," I answered. "In fact, about sixty-three big mistakes. But it's really okay, Mom. I know how to fix them."

"I bet you do, Cassie," she said. "I have a lot of faith in you."

And the weird thing was, she decided to lift my punishment, which meant I could go over to Bess's house and hang out in that blue-sky bedroom and play with Rudy, who still had no manners. And then Bess asked if she could come over to the "unit." That made me nervous, because compared with her house, it was definitely ratty. But she didn't seem to notice; in fact, she actually seemed to like it. She even played chess with Jackson, who practically fell in love with her.

One day we were in my bedroom talking about our next novels. I hadn't exactly given up on my Cat story, but I was stuck at the ending, not knowing what should happen with the King. I needed a big finish, but none of the alternatives (killed the Mystyck Beast/killed *by* the Mystyck Beast/in hiding/in disguise/in disgrace/invisible) made absolute, perfect sense. So I decided to take a little vacation from Cat. I was planning my next heroine, the brilliant and daring Princess Azure.

"Princess Azure. That's a really good name," said Bess. But she was wrinkling her nose in a way I was starting to recognize with her.

"Okay, you hate it."

"No, I don't. Not at all."

"But what?"

"But nothing. I just think, if you want a blue name, Cerulean is better."

"Princess Cerulean? You're kidding, Bess, right?"

"No, I'm not, Cassie. I think Cerulean is excellent."

"Yeah, well, maybe for a boy: 'Prince Cerulean.' 'King Cerulean.' Actually, I sort of like that."

"Well, you can't have it," Bess said, giggling. "It's mine."

I threw my pillow at her. Suddenly I realized Miranda was standing in the doorway, staring at us.

"Yes?" I demanded.

She just stood there with a funny look on her face. Finally she spoke.

"Male," she announced.

"Male caller?" I hadn't heard the phone ring, but now my heart jumped. Was it Danny again? Adam Klein? *Mr. Mullaney?*

"No, Casshead," she said. Then she thrust something toward me. An envelope. I stared at it like a brain-dead moron. "Mail," she repeated. "I got one too. So did Jackson."

"It's from Florida," I said stupidly.

"Why, yes it is. Bravo, Captain Obvious."

"Listen, Cassie, do you want me to leave?" Bess asked.

"No," I said quickly. "Don't."

She nodded, but then she stood up. "Okay. I'll be in the living room."

We watched her walk down the hallway. Then I sat down on my bed.

"Well? Aren't you going to open it?" Miranda asked.

My hands were shaking, but somehow I did.

Dearest Cassie,

It's hard to believe that it's been seven months since I've seen you. They've been the toughest seven months I've ever spent. But

I'm writing to tell you I'm on my way back to Emerson, and I can't wait to see you again.

I have so much to say to you. First, the easy part: I love you. Don't think because you haven't heard from me lately that anything's changed in that department, because it hasn't and it never will. That's a promise.

But now for the harder part: explaining what happened. It's complicated, sweetheart, but it boils down to the fact that I did something very wrong at work, and I told Mom about it, and she was upset. We agreed that we needed time apart to figure things out and that I should speak to you kids in my own words, in my own way. I think she's been incredibly patient, Cassie. Whatever happens between Mom and me, I want you to know that I think she is a special person.

You probably don't understand why you haven't heard more from me. The honest truth is that ever since I left Emerson I've been thinking about what to tell you, and no words ever seemed good enough. But I couldn't let any more time pass without contacting you, so please try not to judge this letter too harshly. I know it isn't great, but of course you're the writer in this family, not me.

Here's to you, O daughter Cassie. See you very soon.

Love,
Dad

When I got to the end, my eyes jumped back to the beginning, then sort of ping-ponged all over the page. "Something very wrong at work," "coming back to Emerson," "what to tell you," Mom's "a special person." What did it all mean? I wasn't sure. I had just about as many unanswered questions as when I opened the envelope.

But for some strange reason I felt happy. Even if it wasn't the absolutely perfect conclusion I was hoping for.

"So, what do you think?" Miranda asked, searching my face.

"I'm not sure," I answered. "I want to hear what he has to say. But I'm glad he's coming back. Are you?"

"I don't know. I guess so. I'm still mad at him, though."

"Me too." It was the first time I'd ever said that, and it surprised me. Then something else occurred to me, and I sprang from my bed and raced down the hall into Jackson's room.

He was sitting on his floor, staring at a chessboard.

"Jackie, did you open that letter just now? The one from Dad?"

He nodded, still staring at the chessboard.

"Do you want me to read it to you?"

"You don't have to, Cassie."

"Really, Jackie boy? Are you sure? Because I will—"

Just then the phone rang. It was Mom, who said she knew about the letters, and she was taking an early train home. So I told Bess the whole story, and she gave me a hug and said she'd probably better be going. By the time Bess left, Miranda was already yakking away on the phone with Madison, telling her the news. So I tossed some potatoes into the oven and *didn't* set the temperature to five hundred degrees, and then I sat down at my insanely cluttered desk.

Maybe I'd work on my Cat story after all, I thought. Maybe it was finally ready to end.

But just when I'd located a black extra-fine-point Rolling Writer, I realized someone was standing in my doorway. It was Jackson, and he was holding something in his hand.

"Cassie? Can I tell you something?" he asked.

I wanted to throttle him, but I didn't. "Yeah. Okay, Jackie. *What?*"

"Guess what," he said, waving a tiny paperback. "Remember *Farmer Joe's Busy Week*?"

"Yes, of course I do. How can I forget?"

"Well, guess what, Cassie. I can *read* it. What a dumb book!"